SEVEN SPIDERS SPINNING

By Gregory Maguire
illustrated by Dirk Zimmer

HarperTrophy
A Division of HarperCollins*Publishers*

Seven Spiders Spinning
Text copyright © 1994 by Gregory Maguire
Illustrations copyright © 1994 by Dirk Zimmer

Printed in the United States of America.
For information address
HarperCollins Children's Books,
a division of HarperCollins Publishers,
10 East 53rd Street, New York, NY 10022.

Published by arrangement with Clarion Books,
a Houghton Mifflin Company imprint.

LC Number 93-30478
Trophy ISBN 0-06-440595-8
First Harper Trophy edition, 1995.

Contents

For my newest nephew and niece,
Patrick Maguire
Elizabeth Maguire
and for the expanding tribe of my godchildren,
actual and honorary:
Aakash Ahamed
Brian Clother
Kate and Maeve Miller Downey
Navida and Nadim Keshavjee
Salim Keshavjee
Conor Clarke McCarthy
Razi and Matin Mirshahi
Emily and Joshua Mock
Brendan O'Brien
Alexandra Olender
Zachary, Alexander, and Michael Pabalan
Jacob, Daniel, Mark, and Erika Savage
Aaleeya, Rehanah, and Tariq Umedaly Spence
Ben, Eli, Theo, and Sam Terris
Robert and Margaret Willison

Spider, spider, in the night,
Dangling by the bathroom light,
Why do you have to bother me
Just when I want some privacy?

Preface: Seven Spiders Spinning

Countless thousands of years ago, give or take a couple of days, a mama spider laid some eggs. She admired them and she rested a little. Then she killed the papa spider, to whom she wasn't deeply attached, and sat down to a satisfying meal. This was not Great Evil. It was in her spider genes. She couldn't help it.

There were seven eggs. In time they hatched, and seven little blind baby spiders began to explore their world. It would be some days before their eyes would open, and when this happened, they would see their devoted mama and fall in love with her, as did all good spider children. But the mama spider went out for a walk and was eaten by a snowy eagle. The bird died of food poisoning a few minutes later. The seven blind baby spiders huddled up against one another, lonely and hungry, waiting for their mama who, alas, would never return.

Later in the day the Ice Age started and the seven spiders were frozen solid in an instant glacier.

Without knowing they were in deep freeze, they waited.

The Ice Age was a good long one. All the rest of their species died out. But our seven spiders were caged in ice. They survived.

Our story continues a thousand years ago, and thousands of miles away, when a Viking sailor named Lars Larsen set out from his home in the tundra with forty-two brave and stalwart sailors. They were trying to find an ocean route from Scandinavia across the Arctic Circle, way up north of Russia, and down to the fragrant spice fields of old Cathay.

Unfortunately, the sea north of Russia is iced over solid for fifty weeks out of every year. Still, Lars Larsen was a plucky guy, and his sailors were loyal. In six years they covered about three hundred ocean miles. In the seventh year, while ice fishing on the frozen ocean, they were lucky to meet a hearty local woman named Hubda the Magnificent. She offered to lead Lars Larsen and his sailors overland to the nearest unfrozen ocean, thousands of miles away. There they could hail a passing coracle to take them to the Orient.

Hubda the Magnificent was a reliable guide. Once, when a terrible blizzard swarmed down on them, she found a cave where the brave band hunkered down for a while. In the cave, frozen to the wall, was a block of ice with the seven spiders in it. Hubda told Lars Larsen and his sailors local legends about spiders from before the dawn of time. How the world had been invented by the spider god. How the spider mother of heaven spun the daylight every spring. How to survive the nasty bites of mythical spiders.

But when Lars Larsen and his sailors wanted to pry the block of frozen spiders out of the wall and take it with them as a souvenir, Hubda the Magnificent paled. She didn't think it a good idea. Maybe the old spider legends were true. She took off one night during a dark howling storm and never returned. We wouldn't know anything about her if it weren't for the ancient poem, *The Epic Verses of Hubda the Magnificent.*

There was something entrancing about the spiders. Their breed would be known in modern times, through fossilized remains, as Siberian snow spiders, or Siberian tarantulas. Their nearest modern relative? *Lycosa tarentula,* or the wolf spider, the bad blood of the family Lycosidae.

Lars and his sailors began to realize they'd never reach Cathay. They turned about and went home, taking the spiders with them. They built a little ice temple in the middle of the village and admired their magical spiders kept on display inside it.

A few years later Lars Larsen again began thinking of cloves and black pepper. He gathered his old crew and sailed west this time.

They brought the frozen spiders in their column of ice as a magic charm to ensure the trip's safety. Alas, the Viking ship crashed into Iceland and sank. Lars Larsen and all hands on deck went down into the cold marble sea.

The block of ice in which the seven Siberian tarantulas were sealed? It bobbed around and bumped around. Baby seals used it for a diving board. Penguins lolled on it. After a while it nudged up against the ice shelf of northern Iceland, was snowed over, and became lost to view.

Until about a thousand years later. A period of global warming caused the ice shelf to snap off and to float, a chunk the size of Manhattan, out into the shipping lanes of the North Atlantic.

There it was noticed, of course. Scientists were airlifted in to do geologic experiments. One of them discovered the Siberian tarantulas in their frozen tomb.

PERFECT PREHISTORIC SPECIMENS! The headlines blurted the news all around the world. The ice floe was hacked into a piece about the size of a combination washer/dryer, packed into a refrigerated crate, and brought by helicopter to Nova Scotia, in Canada.

From there it was to be flown to Harvard University, in Cambridge, Massachusetts. But an air traffic controllers' strike made air delivery unreliable. So the special crate was put on a railroad car and shunted to Montreal. There the crate was lashed to a pallet and loaded onto a truck by husky Canadian teamsters. The truck roared out of Montreal, down through New York, and across the state border into Vermont, heading for Massachusetts. Once, to avoid a cocker spaniel puppy in the road, the driver had to swerve suddenly. He didn't know that the corner of the crate struck the inside of the truck. The crate split open.

And when the crate split open, the refrigeration failed. So after many thousands of years the Siberian snow spiders finally began to defrost.

One of them—hardly larger than a baby mouse—was curious after its long nap. Though still blind, it made its way out of the box and into the driver's cab. It dropped on a thread from the rearview mirror, waving its eight hairy legs in joyful exercise.

The driver, a middle-aged man named Pierre Montrose, had a heart attack on the spot. The truck overturned into a ravine at 9:00 P.M. on a warm Friday night in early September. Its wheels spun for a half hour in the air, and folks in the nearby town of Hamlet, Vermont, came running to see. They pulled the driver from the wreckage and sent him in an ambulance to the hospital in Montpelier.

All that was left of the contents of the crate was a small pool of melted ice.

1: Falling in Love Again

"The meeting of the Tattletales will come to order!"

Seven girls sat up straight on their sleeping bags. Six of them looked still and anxious. The Vermont woods bristled at the far edge of the backyard. Hamlet was a *small* town, and the woods came close. The seventh girl, the one speaking, glanced around in the firelight.

"My name is Thekla Mustard," the speaker began.

"We *know* who you are, we've all been in school together since kindergarten," pointed out Lois.

"*I'm* running this meeting," said Thekla Mustard. "Permission to interrupt and complain and carp and be annoying is not awarded, Lois. *Fermez la bouche.*" This meant *Shut up*, but politely, in French. Lois clamped her mouth shut.

"As you all know, I have been elected Empress of our club for another season. At this our first meeting of the school year, I want to

1

outline the goals and objectives of our club once again. Objections?"

No one spoke. Lois had wanted to be Empress this year, and she popped her gum defiantly, but Thekla chose to pretend it was simply a log snapping in the campfire. The light was golden, the shadows behind them purple and gloomy. As Thekla stood to address the Tattletales, she admitted she cut a magnificent figure in her safari togs complete with pith helmet swathed in muslin. She swayed around the fire to produce a more impressive effect. The tails of her muslin netting trailed poetically behind her.

"School begins next Tuesday," said Thekla Mustard. "The seven of us will find ourselves once again next to our archenemies, our rivals, the bane of our existence: the Copycats."

Thekla fiddled with her veils while the Tattletales spit and fumed and cried, "Boo! Yuck! Scuzz-bombs! Boys stink!"

"Some," said Thekla, "will ask: Why do Copycats exist?"

There was a pause. No one was sure of the rhetorical pattern. "Well, *ask*," Thekla urged, in a whisper.

"Why *do* the Copycats exist?" cried Fawn.

"And well you might ask," said Thekla. "You might as well ask why do spiders exist, and rats, and pond scum, and chicken pox—"

2

"Why *do* spiders exist, and rats, and—" cried Fawn.

"It's a question of the Natural Order," Thekla explained. "In order to be superior, you have to have lower life forms to be superior *to*. A cat is superior to a mouse. A dog is superior to a cat. A girl is superior to a boy."

The girls nodded in righteous agreement and pride, and huddled closer.

"Now, one may wonder what is the goal and objective of our—"

"What *is* the goal and objective of our club anyway?" shrieked Fawn, getting carried away. Thekla delivered a withering frown with her usual effectiveness. Fawn began to bite her fingernails.

Thekla recounted the history of the Copycats and the Tattletales. How the rival clubs were founded several years back. How the name of the Tattletales, applied originally by the boys as an insult, had been taken up by the girls. "Defuse the powers of opposition!" cried Thekla. "*We* own the language, and we transform it! Does the word *tattletales* suggest a clot of simpering namby-pambies, idiotic goody-goody two-shoes, authority-bound *mushbrains?*"

"*Does* the word *tattletales*—" began Fawn, but she was drowned out by the other girls shouting, "NO!"

"Not anymore," Thekla concluded. "The tales we Tattletales tell are the new legends of dominance and power! The tattling we do is to ourselves! Only by self-criticism will we arise to take our rightful place in the corridors of power!"

By this she meant the corridors of the Josiah Fawcett Elementary School.

"Specifically," continued Thekla, "our goal for the next month is to compete against the Copycats in the annual Josiah Fawcett Elementary School Halloween Pageant of Horrors. And we're going to *win*."

She reviewed how the Tattletales had won first prize for horror the year before. The six girls sat agog in pleasurable glory: Lois, Fawn, Carly, Nina, Sharday, and Anna Maria.

What the girls didn't know was that the seven baby Siberian snow spiders, attracted by the warmth of the campfire, had scrabbled through the underbrush of the forest toward them.

Like all babies, the spiders were impressionable. They wanted warmth and affection. Each one of the seven spiders, crouching in the weeds, warmed by the heat of the campfire, opened its eyes at last. Each one cast its eyes on the seven girls. Each spider picked out a girl to be its mother. This is called imprinting. Baby ducklings can think a farm dog is their mother. Sheepdogs can form filial bonds with shepherds. Each of these tarantulas, left over from the Ice Age, fell in love with its own Tattletale.

2: The Copycats Gather

Across town, in a tree house built across the generous boughs of two adjacent trees, the rival club was having its own first meeting of the season.

The leader was Sammy Grubb. He was hanging upside down by his knees from a branch fifty feet above the ground. His friends and fellow Copycats were similarly treed: Hector, Stanislaus, Mike, Salim, Moshe, and Forest Eugene. They were reading comic books, trading Monsters of the Universe cards, having long-distance spitting contests, or leafing through the *Science Times*. The tree house was in Sammy Grubb's backyard. The smell of dying charcoal briquettes drifted up from the grill.

"Sammy Grubb!" called his mom from the deck. "If you fall out of that tree and scramble your IQ, so help me I'll brain you!"

Sammy was embarrassed, but he swung right side up and said, "Okay, guys, let's get to work."

The boys hunkered down. "We're all here.

School starts on Tuesday," said Sammy. "We've got the best teacher in creation, Miss Earth, for the second year in a row. Only one trouble stands in our way."

"And what might that be?" asked Salim, who had just moved to Hamlet, Vermont, from the subcontinent of India.

"The upcoming threat to our winning first prize in the Halloween Pageant of Horrors," said Sammy Grubb. "The Tattletales. The annual Josiah Fawcett Elementary School Halloween Pageant of Horrors is upon us. We have only seven weeks to plan and execute a five-minute play that will terrorize everyone in the school and win us first prize for the scariest skit."

"Who won last year?" asked Salim.

"Well, it was unfair—" began Moshe, but Sammy said, "The girls did. We went on first, with a Frankenstein rap. Forest Eugene wrote it."

Forest Eugene leapt up and began:

I'm the king of second-hand hearts!
Made of other folks' spare parts!
Nothing that I've got is mine!
Ain't no original Frankenstein!
Every extra bit of you,
Fingernails or earwax glue,
Makes me up! So I'm your chap!
Let's all do the Frankenstein rap!

"Well, that's pretty neat," said Salim. "What did the girls come up with?"

Moshe said sadly, "Somehow they got wind of what we were up to. Spying, of course. They're great spies. They did a Frankenstein's bride routine. They ended it with a chorus line of high-kicking Frankenstein's brides, singing 'There's No Business Like Show Business.' It wasn't even an original song."

"It *was* funny," said Hector. "Those high kicks, and all that big hair."

"Traitor," grumbled Stanislaus.

"The point is this," said Sammy. "We must come up with an original idea this year. Any suggestions?"

"A Monster Beauty Contest!" said Mike.

"No, that's the Tattletales on a regular day," said Moshe.

"A Dracula Drag Race, with soapbox derby cars?" said Stanislaus.

"Hmmm. Maybe," said Sammy Grubb, meaning: No.

"How about this?" said Forest Eugene. "The papers have been full of this discovery of prehistoric spiders. They've been reporting about this ancient Russian poem called *The Epic Verses of Hubda the Magnificent.* The Hubda verses tell the legend of the mythical spider-beasts of the Arctic. We could write a play about it. We could call it *My Fair Hubda.*"

"Possibly," said Sammy. "Spiders are always good for the jitters."

The meeting adjourned shortly. Sammy Grubb went in and helped his mom dry the dishes while Sammy's dad had a beer and repaired the screens on the back door. Sammy's dad didn't notice the shape in the forsythia bushes, a shape remarkably like a girl, slip back into the shadows and disappear.

3: Six Spiders Witness a Kidnapping

The spiders were warm and snug. They had built a seven-layer web in a triangular patch of tangled ravine in the woods known locally as Foggy Hollow. Small bugs, a bat, and a family outing of moths fluttered in, got stuck, and were wound up in tarantula threads for a tasty midnight snack.

Luckily nobody walked in the woods of Foggy Hollow. Or not usually. But tonight, as the full moon rose, a girl was making her way home. *She* had been the girl-shaped shadow outside Sammy Grubb's house. Her name was Pearl Hotchkiss, and she was the only student in Miss Earth's class not to belong to any club.

Pearl was smart, brave, kind, and most of all, independent. She liked the girls in her class, she just didn't like clubs. She also liked the boys in her class, but she knew better than to say so aloud. Even if the boys invited her to join, she wouldn't. She just didn't like clubs.

So she was on her way home from the supermarket, where she'd been buying zipper-top sandwich bags and baloney to make lunches for school, when she happened to glide past Sammy Grubb's backyard. She liked Sammy Grubb. She heard the boys planning a play about Siberian snow spiders. She thought it was a good idea.

Then she took a shortcut through Foggy Hollow. At home, her parents and her younger sisters—lots of them—and her baby brother were waiting for her. Pearl knew the woods well, and the moon was as bright as fireworks. She wasn't scared of bears, or bats. But when she got to the spiderwebs, she stopped.

"Yikes," said Pearl. "This makes that video *Arachnophobia* look like a nursery rhyme."

She went up a little closer. The spiders were like knots of hairy twine, delicately twitching, dark clots of bristle and velvet gliding across their webs. "Well, what do you know?" said Pearl out loud, to give herself courage. "Those are the biggest spiders I ever saw."

She remembered Sammy Grubb's Halloween pageant idea of the spider-beasts. Pearl didn't care to get involved in the stupid battle between Tattletales and Copycats. But she didn't mind if Sammy Grubb liked her a little.

"Surely there'll be some sort of show-and-tell the first week of school," said Pearl, talking herself into a feat of courage. "Miss Earth did it last year. She loves show-and-tell. I could bring a spider. I could pretend it was a Siberian snow spider. . . ."

Pearl opened the box of zipper-top plastic sandwich bags and took one out. It was just the right size for carrying a spider from Foggy Hollow. But how could she tempt the spider inside? Then she remembered the baloney. She opened the paper wrapping, took out a slice, and rolled it attractively into a cocktail snack, like a cigar. She stuck a twig through it, toothpick-style, and pushed the meat into the bottom of the plastic bag. Tiptoeing toward the nearest web, she murmured softly, "Here, spidey-widey." At the base of the shivering web she left the bag and backed off.

The nearest spider trembled with interest. It showed restraint and patience at first. But then, with a brushing of its legs you could almost hear, it scurried inside the bag and hugged the baloney as if it had found a new friend.

Pearl Hotchkiss used a long stick to press the lips of the plastic bag together. When it was safely closed, she poked a few holes in the bag for air. No point bringing a dead spider to school, however gloriously hairy and scary it was.

The spider embracing the baloney hardly

seemed to notice being lifted up and carried away. Its six relatives, however, were rigid with attention. As the moon rose higher and higher, and they began to realize the seventh spider wasn't coming back, they all met in one web and traced out lines with their delicate spinnerets. If one didn't know any better, one would think they were hatching a plan to rescue their poor, kidnapped sibling.

4: Show-and-Tell

Miss Earth smiled at her class. Such good children they were! She took her first attendance of the year.

"Salim Bannerjee," she said, "you're the new boy. Welcome to our school."

"Yes, Miss Earth. Thank you, Miss Earth."

"Nina Bueno?"

"Here, Miss Earth."

"Moshe Cohn?"

"At your service, Miss Earth."

"Carly Garfunkel?"

"Present and accounted for, Miss Earth."

"Sammy Grubb?"

"I'm your main man, Miss Earth."

"Pearl Hotchkiss?"

"At your beck and call, Miss Earth."

"Lois Kennedy the Third?"

"Ready and waiting, Miss Earth."

"Anna Maria Mastrangelo?"

"Your willing slave, Miss Earth."

"Forest Eugene Mopp?"

"With abject devotion, Miss Earth."

"Thekla Mustard?"

"Wouldn't miss this for the world, Miss Earth."

"Fawn Petros?"

"Swinging from a star, Miss Earth."

"Michael St. Michael?"

"Rocking 'round the clock, Miss Earth."

"Stanislaus Tomaski?"

"Singing in the rain, Miss Earth."

"Hector Yellow?"

"Fly me to the moon, Miss Earth."

"Sharday Wren?"

"Your love keeps lifting me higher than I ever been lifted before, Miss Earth."

"Well," said Miss Earth, beaming, "it's nice to be back together, isn't it, class?" The children smiled pleasantly at their beloved teacher. Then she turned her back to write *What I Did on My Summer Vacation* on the blackboard. Immediately a storm of spitballs, notes, paper airplanes, rubber bands from orthodontic braces, and early bits of lunch erupted across the room. Thekla Mustard quickly distributed a photocopied announcement of the next meeting to the girls in the Tattletales club, slipping back into her seat again just in time. Miss Earth turned back to the children. The class was still, hands folded on desktops. Fifteen smiles, made more beautiful by toothpaste with fluoride, flashed like spotlights on her. It made her feel quite dizzy for a moment. "How I do love teaching," she murmured. "It transports you to paradise."

"Yes, we're sure it does, Miss Earth," they agreed.

Miss Earth said, "Later on, my little cub reporters, we'll do the traditional paragraph on how we spent our summer vacations— adventures, family outings, goals achieved, new habits formed, pets run over by cars, that sort of thing—but for now I would like our new student, Salim Bannerjee, to tell us a little bit about himself. Our first contributor to show-and-tell this year, if you please?"

Salim stood. He was a formal boy. "My dear Miss Earth. Boys and girls. With my mom and dad I moved to Hamlet, Vermont, last month. My mom has a job at Locust Computer Labs, a few miles away in New Hampshire—"

"So does my dad! So does my mom!" chorused about two thirds of the class, cheerfully. The presence of Locust Computer Labs was one reason Hamlet, Vermont, was so well supplied with children from so many different backgrounds.

"I became friends with Moshe, who introduced me to Sammy Grubb," said Salim. "And I have joined a club called the Copycats."

Miss Earth sighed. "Oh dear. I'd hoped to persuade you not to join—"

"But why ever not, Miss Earth?"

"I believe that clubs are hostile and exclusionary," said Miss Earth. "I know no one in this room agrees with me, except Pearl Hotchkiss." But Pearl was busy watching her

16

spider in its plastic-bag cage in her desk, and she didn't say anything.

Thekla Mustard raised her hand and was given permission to speak. "With all due respect, Miss Earth," she said, "since I am Empress of the Tattletales—the foremost high-class club in this community—it falls to me to utter a word of rebuttal."

"And what might that word be?" asked Miss Earth. "What *are* clubs, if not divisive, mean-spirited, and corrosive of the social fabric?"

Thekla Mustard said, snappily, "Fun." And all the children except Pearl cheered.

Miss Earth remarked, "Fun for some but not for all. But more of this later. Salim, have you anything more to add?"

"I am happy to be here," he said.

"And we're happy to know you. Now, who would like to show-and-tell next?"

Pearl Hotchkiss raised her hand. She was motioned to the front of the room, where she stood with the plastic bag hidden behind her back.

"I would like to tell about Siberian snow spiders," she said. "The ones they discovered in the Arctic Circle in August. I believe I have captured one."

"How could you have captured one?" said Sammy Grubb. "Aren't they at Harvard, being studied by grad students?"

"This one escaped," said Pearl. She thought she

was lying. She didn't know how true it was. "I found it in Foggy Hollow. It lives on baloney sandwiches with mustard; it seems to prefer French Dijon mustard made with white wine. My studies are incomplete on that point, however. It is full of poison, so nobody do anything sneaky. Or I can't answer for the consequences."

She drew the bag out from behind her back. The class gasped. Miss Earth drew her attractive feet up onto the rungs of her chair. The boys shivered. The girls whistled. Sammy Grubb's mouth dropped open. Thekla Mustard's mouth clamped shut. The spider flexed its hairy legs and made the plastic envelope pulse up and down. The spider looked about the size of a golf ball. "Mother Nature at her most grotesque," breathed Pearl. She was watching Sammy Grubb and enjoying his attention.

"What can anyone tell us about these so-called Siberian snow spiders?" asked Miss Earth faintly.

Forest Eugene raised his hand. "I read in the *Science Times* that little is known about them. They probably come from a branch of the spider family that died off a long time ago. No one really knows if they're poisonous or not, not yet. I keep looking at the papers to see what the scientists at Harvard say, but the spiders seem to have dropped out of the news since last week."

"Please be very careful with this spider," said Miss Earth, motioning Pearl away from the front of the room with a gracious smile. "We wouldn't want any catastrophes. But I am curious why you think it is one of the famous Siberian snow spiders."

"Well," said Pearl, "it's my guess the spider fell out of the airplane carrying it to Harvard." She didn't want to say there were six more where she found this one, for that would make her spider less special.

"Hey, look," said Sammy. "The spider seems to have spotted a friend."

Very true. Pearl's show-and-tell was lurching against its bag. It had caught sight of Nina, with whom it had fallen in love a few days earlier. At the time, the spider hadn't dared leave its family to follow Nina in love and devotion. But now—it was separated from its siblings anyway. Though well supplied with baloney, it was imprisoned and lonely, and the sight of Nina caused its little spider heart to swell with joy. It tried to rip its way out of the bag.

"Yuck," said Nina, moving away. "I don't want such a friend, no-siree."

"Don't worry," said Pearl. "I wouldn't let it loose, Nina. It might try to kiss you and accidentally bite you. Then it would be curtains for Nina."

Pearl didn't know how right she was.

She put the bag carefully inside an old Muppets lunch box, into which she had pounded air holes through the eyes of Kermit and Miss Piggy. The whole class breathed a sigh of relief to have the spider out of sight. The spider, inside the plastic inside the Muppets lunch box, however, scrabbled with grief against its prison and dreamed of escape and joining its one true love, Nina Bueno.

"Wow, Pearl," whispered Sammy Grubb, "you're brave."

"Oh, it was nothing," said Pearl in an off-hand way. But inside she blushed with joy that he had admired her courage.

5: A-Hunting We Will Go

In the damp, still weather of Foggy Hollow, the six Siberian snow spiders were thriving. Every day they napped, strengthened and repaired their webs, and ate what insects and such they could trap. Instinct thousands of years old awoke in them, fresh as the day they were born. The spiders knew a lot about when to be motionless. When to pounce. When to pull their legs under them and look like tufted buttons. When to drop down on a silken line and examine what might lie beneath. When to scrabble back up for safety.

No doubt about it. They were talented tarantulas.

Their genes had trained them to survive in a world of snow and ice. Instead they were growing up in a warm Indian summer in Vermont. Around them leaves began to flush gold and bushes were lavish with crimson. The sun didn't make it all the way into Foggy Hollow, not with that broad canopy of oaks and sugar maples arching overhead, and a good thing too: the spiders weren't well equipped to deal with bright light. The moist, coolish air of Foggy Hollow was just right for toddling spiders. And so they grew and prospered.

They played games, in a sense, little games of spider tag. Which can drop from the branch on its thread fastest? They napped, secure in one another's comforting hairy legs, each dreaming of its favorite Tattletale. But they also remembered their missing sibling spider, and they worried. And while ordinary spiders wouldn't give one another the time of day, the tarantulas from the frozen North had strange and complex memory patterns. In their own arachnoid way, they mourned the loss of their companion. And they each knew that *they* wouldn't be caught waltzing into a plastic bag after a piece of baloney. It just wasn't worth it.

There was a sort of pecking order among the spiders. The one who'd dared to explore Pearl Hotchkiss's plastic bag had been the senior, and the other six understood in which order of importance the rest came, much as a pack of dogs does. The boss of the six remaining spiders was in a small way more advanced than the others.

One evening toward the end of September, the senior of the six touched the spinnerets of the younger five tenderly. It seemed to be saying good-bye. The younger five nuzzled it with rare spiderish emotion, not seen much outside of the best of children's books.

Was the spider setting out to locate and rescue its missing sibling, or was it determined to seek out its own beloved Tattletale and give her a little love bite? No one can say. But in the refreshing cool of midnight the spider took its leave. More by luck than by good sense or planning, it meandered under cover of darkness up the side of Foggy Hollow and toward the town of Hamlet, Vermont. It might have strayed back toward the highway from which it had come and there been squished by traffic. It might have wandered toward Old Man Fingerpie's farm and been trampled on by a cow. If either of these things had happened, the story would have been very different. But by chance, or maybe by a sixth sense, the spider pattered a mile and a half, and when the school buses began to arrive in the morning, it was safely hidden inside the schoolyard bell.

6: Anna Maria Sings a High C

On the blackboard Miss Earth wrote the day's schedule.

Fractions
Spelling Quiz
The Land and People of Russia
Recess: Playground if dry
Reading Aloud: Two chapters of *Matilda* by
  R. Dahl
Current Events
Lunch: Cheese pizza and carrot sticks
Writing a Business Letter
Planning Time: Halloween Pageant
Greek Myths
Quiet Reading Time
Dismissal

While the class groaned over numerators and denominators, the spider in the school bell gradually came to its senses. It had been driven permanently deaf by the alarm clatter at 8:45 when the bell rang. It felt itself all over to make sure it wasn't dead. Then it slipped out of the red iron bell and wobbled across the brick walls of the Josiah Fawcett Elementary School.

The class labored at a spelling quiz. Anna Maria Mastrangelo puzzled over the word *poison*. You had to use it in a sentence. "The spider's bite was full up with poysen," she wrote, and looked at it, unsure, and continued scribbling, "and the rich pretty movie star screamed AAAAAAUGH, POISAN, POYSEN, POISSEN! as she fell to her death among the thorns of Hollywood." There, that should do it.

The spider moved from light fixture to light fixture along the corridor. It bypassed the morning kindergarten class. It peeped in at Mrs. Cobble, the school secretary, but passed her by. It headed for Miss Earth's class at the end of the hall.

"Now who can find Russia on the map?" said Miss Earth. "I'll give you a hint. It's hard to miss."

Various students came up and used the pointer to guess. "No," said Miss Earth. "That's Brazil. No, that's the American Protectorate of Guam. No, that's Antarctica. No, that's Long Island in New York State, Forest Eugene, *really*. No that's—let's see—that's Singapore. Give you another hint. It's the color of Halloween."

Only one country ran for sixteen inches across the map, like a clump of orange pie dough being rolled out from side to side. Everyone got it right away with that clue.

"Now, who can tell me what Russia is famous for?" asked Miss Earth.

Hands went swaying hypnotically like an underwater patch of reeds. Miss Earth called on various students. "Ballet dancers!" "Communism!" "Beet soup!" "Baba Yaga!" "Potatoes and vodka!" "Tsars and czars!" "No toilet paper in the stores!" "Being our enemy but now they're our friend!" "The unsurpassed genius of Peter Ilich Tchaikovsky, whose music for *The Nutcracker Suite* has become an indelible part of the culture of childhood." "Wolves, and throwing people out of sleighs!"

"Very good," said Miss Earth, "if a trifle thin." She began to lecture on the history of the Russian peoples. A couple of students took notes. Everyone else looked out the window at the kindergartners having their morning break. No one saw the spider climb upside down into the room, over the top of the door frame, and come to rest on the portrait of George Washington, where it sat on his head like a splendid 3-D toupee.

At recess the children burst shrieking through the door. The Tattletales and the

Copycats instantly had a relay race. The Tattletales won by two full lengths. The Copycats slithered away in shame and went to play Jump in the Leaves to console themselves.

After recess the spider was more alert. When Anna Maria Mastrangelo filed in with her classmates, the spider sensed her. It looked down. She was wearing an orange sweatshirt and her hair was in little twists. She wanted to be a singing nun when she grew up. The spider swelled with love and crawled along the ceiling to get a little closer.

All the while Miss Earth read *Matilda*, the class sat and drew pictures, listening and sometimes laughing at the funny story. Anna Maria drew a picture of herself as a nun with her own TV special. Her black gown with the white paper bib was ornamented with rhinestone cowboy decorations. The spider peered from the light. It didn't know what nuns were, or rhinestones. But it knew Anna Maria was the genuine article. She was the reason for existence. And more likely than not, tasty. The spider longed to give her a friendly little love nip, to show its undying loyalty. The poison it didn't know it had went surging through its tiny system.

The spider descended on its thread. Had anyone looked up, they would have seen it dropping slowly, slowly, like a slow-motion skydiving hamster. Above the head of Anna Maria it hung, in mute adoration.

Anna Maria noticed a shadow on her drawing. It was blotting out the face of the singing nun. Anna Maria waved her left hand absentmindedly around her head. The air currents swayed the spider a bit. Anna Maria sharpened her pencil, studying her drawing. She ground the lead to an excruciatingly fine point, sharp as a tack. When it was all done, she held the pencil up before her face and squinted with one eye to admire the precision of its perfect point.

With perfectly awful timing, it was at just this second that the spider chose to drop on its thread in front of her. It skewered itself on the needlelike point, right through the chest cavity. Anna Maria screamed and flung the pencil and its glob of hairy something across the room. Over the heads of her classmates sailed the pencil and the paralyzed spider. No one saw exactly what it was, but they all saw it zoom out the window like a velvet candy apple. It landed in the path of a school bus backing up with its backing-up beepers on.

Miss Earth said, "Anna Maria, whatever has gotten into you?"

"I don't know," said Anna Maria, and, shivering with unnamed terror, she screamed again, just to get it out of her system.

"That's a high C," said Thekla brightly. "Anna Maria, perhaps you'll make a singing nun after all. You've given me an idea for the Halloween Pageant of Horrors!"

In the parking lot, the newly sharpened pencil was now splintered to smithereens, and the spider was nothing more than a dark smoosh on the blacktop.

7: Five Little Spiders Weeping on a Web

After lunch that day Miss Earth taught her class how to write business letters. Each student practiced on an imaginary businessperson. Pearl Hotchkiss wrote:

> Pearl Hotchkiss
> Hamlet, Vermont
> September 30

Master Sammy Grubb
Leader, the Copycats
Miss Earth's Class
Josiah Fawcett Elementary School
Hamlet, Vermont

Dear Master Grubb,

I understand you and your Copycat friends are planning a skit involving spiders for the annual Halloween Pageant of Horrors. May I help? I have caught a rare Siberian snow spider, as you may remember. I would be delighted.

> Sincerely,
>
> Pearl Hotchkiss

Pearl examined her authentic-looking business signature with pleasure. It looked like hair collected from the bath drain: just right. She then folded the letter into a paper airplane and delivered it to Sammy Grubb. Airmail.

Sammy felt the missile drive into the back of his head. He read the business letter. He nodded at Pearl solemnly.

A few minutes later, Miss Earth said, "Now, my precious little trinkets, it's time to plan for the Halloween Pageant of Horrors. As you know, most classrooms do a single skit involving all students, I know you want to do two skits instead. I'm not a dictator, so I'll abide by our vote, but I would like to advise you to work together this year rather than divide into clubs." She lectured them briefly on the value of cooperation. Then they voted, students and teacher alike.

The vote came fifteen to one. The students (including Pearl) all voted for separate skits, and Miss Earth for a single one. You had to live with the minuses as well as the pluses of democracy, so Miss Earth sighed and admitted defeat. But she said Pearl Hotchkiss had to be included in one skit or the other. Sammy Grubb spoke up and said that he had invited Pearl to join the Copycats skit.

The room became noisy with desks scraped across the floor into circles. Miss Earth sat at her desk creating prizewinning lesson plans for the weeks to come. The Tattletales listened to Thekla Mustard, and the Copycats to Sammy Grubb.

"Girls," said Thekla, "and I may, without fear of insult, call you girls as you are all minors in a legal sense—though you loom large in my affections, it goes without saying—"

"Then don't say it," wisecracked Lois, dangerously.

"*Girls,*" Thekla went on, "Anna Maria's silver-throated shriek has given me an idea for the Halloween Pageant of Horrors. Now you tell me. What's the scariest thing on earth?"

"Homework?" said Fawn.

"Boys?" said Carly.

"Pit bulls with attitude?" said Sharday.

"Those are *presences,*" said Thekla. "Think of absence. Who in the world could you not live *without?*"

The girls thought. Though they loved their parents dearly, they didn't think they would die without them. The girls wondered if Thekla wanted a fond chorus of "Thekla Mustard!" But before they could muster up the glee necessary for such a display, Anna Maria figured it out.

"Miss Earth!" she hissed.

Their lovely teacher lifted her head. "Yes, Anna Maria?"

"I didn't want your attention, Miss Earth, I was just saying 'Miss Earth,' Miss Earth."

"That's my name, don't wear it out," said

Miss Earth, but she was smiling; it was a joke. She went back to her work.

Thekla nodded with an executive scowl. "You've got it, Anna Maria. Let me explain. I was thinking ghosts, I was thinking ghostesses, and when you screamed in class today, I thought: *in situ*! On location! A classroom tableau! We could do a short skit, 'The Haunting of Miss Earth'! Anna Maria, you could play Miss Earth in her classroom, haunted by the ghosts of former students who couldn't bear to graduate from her blessed classroom, and who writhe in lonely torment for all time, missing her!"

"This is only her second year teaching," Lois pointed out.

"This is *art*," said Thekla firmly. "We take liberties. Anna Maria, do you think you could learn an aria of undying teacherly dedication if I can find one in opera literature?"

"Yes," said Anna Maria. You didn't say no to Thekla Mustard, unless you were Lois Kennedy the Third, who was bold and brazen.

The Tattletales hunkered down to fine-tune their plan. There was only a month before the pageant.

Across the room, the Copycats were hatching their own idea. Forest Eugene Mopp knew of a toy that cooked gloppy rubber spiders in its own little oven. Pearl Hotchkiss's dad worked for a toy distributor. Maybe he could get them one of those ovens! They could do a spider skit, the seven Copycats dressed up as spider-boys, and have rubber spiders on strings. Maybe Sammy's dad, who was good with lumber and nails, could help them build a large web out of knotted rope. The boys could swarm up and down the web singing "My Fair Hubda." And then Pearl Hotchkiss could come onstage dressed in black, led by her gorgeous real spider on a leash! The Spirit of Hubda the Siberian Snow Spider Specialist! Kids would think it was one of the plastic spiders come to life!

Pearl didn't much like the idea of being onstage. She wasn't a showy person. But Sammy Grubb seemed so enthusiastic, so happy that she had offered to help, and he smiled at her in a devastating, thoughtless way. "I'll do it," said Pearl. What's gotten into me? she asked herself.

That evening, as the sun made the western sky look pink as smoked salmon, the five remaining tarantulas came together on one web. They quivered with alarm. Now two of their company were gone, with no sign of returning. You had to feel sorry for the hairy little monsters. They hadn't asked to be frozen for all those years and then carted several thousand miles. They hadn't chosen to be poisonous; they didn't even know they were. Life was

34

hard. In the way that spiders can (or at any rate Siberian snow spiders, a rare and advanced breed), they wept for the mysteries of life.

Around midnight, the senior spider lifted its head bravely into the chilly moist air. Something like grief seemed to surge through its sensitive frame. It gestured a poignant farewell to its poisonous partners and set out to find the missing two tarantulas, or die in the attempt.

8: Spider Sandwich for Sharday

Moshe Cohn was giving a science report. He stood in front of the classroom with a sheet of notes in his hand.

"My report is about Siberian snow spi—" he began.

"Louder, please," sang out Miss Earth from the back of the room. "Ancient ears like mine, ruined by rock and roll, need you to speak up."

Moshe hated public speaking. He started over in a normal voice. "My report is about—"

"*Louder* please!" shrieked all the kids, though they could hear perfectly well. Then they turned and grinned at Miss Earth. To receive her gratitude was heaven. She nodded politely and cupped a hand around her ear.

Moshe took a deep breath. "SIBERIAN SNOW SPIDERS. WHO ARE THEY? WHAT DO THEY WANT?"

"Bravo," said Thekla snootily, though it was none of her beeswax.

Moshe went on in a normal voice. "A mystery surrounds the so-called Siberian snow spider.

Strictly speaking, the beast is an arachnid, not an overgrown insect, since like all members of the spider family it has eight legs. Last night on TV, Meg Snoople, the investigative news reporter, did a segment on the spiders. They were found in a block of ice in the Atlantic Ocean in August, but now it's October and no word has come out of Harvard University about them. Meg Snoople and her camera crew went to Cambridge and pestered the scientists. It was great! She rushed through the double doors of a science hall lecture theater. The cameras pulled back dramatically when she thrust a microphone into the face of a professor and shouted, 'The spiders, Professor Williams! Where are they? America demands to know!'"

In Miss Earth's classroom, sixteen beings hung slack-jawed to hear the answer: the estimable Miss Earth, Pearl Hotchkiss, seven Tattletales, the six other Copycats, and the exploring tarantula who had left the web two nights earlier.

This spider was more cautious than the other two. The creature had followed the trail of its older sibling, leaf to leaf, twig to telephone pole, lawn to hedge to road to roadside vegetable stand. And so to the Josiah Fawcett Elementary School, where it avoided the red school bell out of a healthy suspicion. Or maybe it picked up bad spider vibes.

It was now poised with its filament-furred legs drawn up against its body, crouched on the very tip of the flagpole. The spider did not, could not, understand English, but it seemed impressed by Moshe's delivery.

For dramatic effect Moshe switched approaches. "Now most tarantulas," he said, leaving the class breathless to learn what Professor Williams had answered to Meg Snoople, "most tarantulas don't build webs, except for certain types from South America. Tarantulas are of the family Teraphosidae (order Araneida). They were called tarantulas after the town of Taranto, Italy, where people used to think that a bite from one would make you hop about and cry buckets and fling yourself into a wild dance complete with tambourines decorated with colored ribbons." Moshe put his paper down. "They named a dance after this sickness, called the tarantella. Ta-ran-TEL-la. Sounds like a different way of saying ta-RAN-choo-la, doesn't it? I've asked a fellow student to demonstrate."

Grinning, Sharday Wren slid from her seat. Moshe was too shy to dance the tarantella in public. And Sharday took tap dance and modern. Thekla and some of the other Tattletales were scandalized that Sharday would help a

Copycat with his report. Of course boys were feeble, and mentally they developed much more slowly than *girls*, everyone knew that. But this was still no reason for betrayal.

Still, Sharday Wren danced a mean tarantella. Her legs lifted in stylish arcs, and the tambourine went bang-bang-banging from her hip to the heel of her palm. Everyone in the room was mesmerized. The spider especially.

Sharday was its own true love.

Sharday was the first creature it had laid eyes on when it awoke. It had come to true love with great energy and single-mindedness. Sharday was everything to it. The spider swooned and nearly fell off the flag. It forgot all about searching for its missing family members. It throbbed with passion. Its only aim in life was to fling itself into the delighted presence of its ladylove. If it could have sung, it would have made up a top ten hit called "Sharday."

When she was done, Sharday sat back down in her chair. Moshe continued with his report. "Now, on the news last night, when Meg Snoople asked her nosy question and raised her eyebrows in interest, Professor Williams could only mutter and stammer something about 'Minor difficulties—Is this off the record?—No comment—I would've worn my tweed jacket with the leather patches and brought my pipe—But I wonder if I could have

39

your autograph for my daughter before you go
. . . ?' At which Meg Snoople turned and said to
the camera, and all of America, 'There's more
to this than meets the eye. Stay tuned,
America, I'll snoop till I droop! When we come
back we'll have tips on ten ways to beautify
your mailbox for under a dollar.' The Professor
was taking out a pen for the autograph when
the show ended, and that's the end of my
report too."

Moshe sat down to well-deserved applause.
Then the lunch bell rang. Miss Earth reminded
everyone that because the cafeteria was having
its ceiling repaired they had to eat in their
classroom. She was sure they'd behave for the
lunch lady, Mrs. Brill. She then left to have her
own nutritious low-fat yogurt and apple juice,
and a chocolate-coconut doughnut for dessert.

Moshe and Sharday were sitting next to each
other. Overhead the spider gazed down from
the flag. Moshe said, "Thanks, Sharday. You're
a great dancer."

"Welcome. Good report, Moshe. What do
you have for lunch?"

Moshe checked the bag. "A bagel and lox,
two slices of dill pickle, a can of cream soda, a
Jaffa orange peeled and segmented, and a
Reese's Peanut Butter Cup for dessert. How
about you?"

Sharday's mom wrapped her lunch in old-fashioned wax paper. She had to unwrap it to see. She even had to take the lid off the sandwich. In a huge clump in the middle of the bread was a dollop of egg salad. "I like to spread it out myself," said Sharday. "I'm a fussy eater. Where's the plastic knife she usually packs? Mrs. Brill! Mrs. Brill! My mom forgot to pack my plastic knife!"

"The horror, the horror," said Mrs. Brill. "Come here and let me see what I have in my bag that'll do."

Sharday left the sandwich open on her desk. But Moshe had a Swiss Army knife, and to thank Sharday for dancing so neatly he quickly whipped it out and slathered the egg salad to the edges. He picked up the top slice of bread and turned to the front of the room. "There you are, Sharday, I've done it for you."

"Thank heavens, the nearest I was coming to a plastic knife was a tongue depressor," said Mrs. Brill. "Sharday, go eat your lunch now."

The spider let itself down on a line and landed on the gooey carpet of egg salad. No one saw it. "Don't smush the bread together, I hate that!" Sharday was saying to Moshe. "I told you, I'm *fussy*!"

"I won't, I'm not, I didn't," Moshe said, setting the bread down gently. The top slice seemed to sit rather higher off the bottom than he might have guessed, but maybe this was gourmet egg salad. He went back to his own lunch.

Sharday sat down. She picked up her sandwich and opened her mouth.

"How can you eat?" said a voice from the next desk. "How can you go on as if everything were normal?"

From between the two slices of bread the spider focused its eyes on Sharday, eight inches away. But she didn't see it. She was looking at Thekla Mustard.

"I have half a mind to vote to suspend you from Tattletales," said Thekla sharply. "Helping Moshe Cohn with his report!"

"Just because I belong to a club doesn't mean I am your slave, Thekla," said Sharday. "All I did was dance a dance I already knew how to dance."

"Are we disgusted? Girls, *are* we?" asked Thekla. There were grunts of moderate vagueness.

Lois Kennedy the Third said, "Oh, Thekla, you're only jealous because you can't dance to save your life."

Moshe said, "It was a good dance, Sharday. I already said so. That doesn't mean you can be a Copycat or anything."

"Well, really," said Thekla, "if I must stand alone in my disdain, so be it. I have never minded staking out the highest moral ground, though it is a lonely position sometimes."

Sharday's mouth was still opened to bite. But a noisy argument erupted between Copycats and Tattletales. Sharday set her sandwich down. She was steaming with fury. When the bell rang for playground, she got up to leave. "Eat your lunch, Sharday," cried Mrs. Brill, but Sharday said, "I'm too upset, I couldn't eat a thing," and ran out of the classroom.

Mrs. Brill hadn't brought a lunch. She thought she might take a little nibble of Sharday's chunky-looking sandwich. But just as she headed toward it, the janitor came through with his portable trash masher and scooped up all the leftover lunches. The spider never knew what hit it.

9: Four Spiders Hold a Council of War

Nurse Prudence Lark had been working at the Montpelier Community Hospital for many years. In all that long and worthy career, no patient had ever touched her heart as deeply as the poor truck driver from Canada.

Pierre Montrose lay in a coma, his legs in traction, his neck in a brace, his thoughts on hold. When Nurse Lark had an extra few minutes she loved to scurry to his room and sit by his side. He had no family, but Nurse Lark knew that coma patients sometimes responded well to the sound of the human voice.

So Nurse Lark, who was a little lonely herself, talked to Pierre Montrose. She read him her favorite romance novel, *Love's Tender Torture*. She imagined she saw him cry a little when she read the part about the hero's suicide leap. She read to him from *People* magazine. She read to him from the newspaper,

Dear Abby especially. He seemed to like Dear Abby. He twitched less than usual.

Nurse Lark's boss, Head Nurse Crisp, didn't approve of all this attention.

"But he's alone in a foreign land!" said Nurse Lark. "He has no friends! I can't just let him lie there and rot."

Head Nurse Crisp brisked through the charts. "Put on the TV," she said. "That'll have to do. A professional nurse does not fall in love with an unshaven coma patient, Nurse Lark," she said pointedly. "What did happen to this Monsieur Montrose anyway?"

"His truck overturned on the interstate," said Nurse Lark. "About five weeks ago. He had a heart attack and a concussion at the same time. His heart is fine now, all healed up, good as new. But what could bring him out of his coma?"

"True love?" said Head Nurse Crisp with a blank expression.

"Maybe," breathed Nurse Lark, pushing back her graying curls and looking at the patient tenderly.

"Dream on." Head Nurse Crisp sailed away, laughing nastily. "You have a soap-opera idea of life, Nurse Lark! Beware it!"

Nurse Lark couldn't disobey her boss. And there were lots of other patients who needed her attention. But on her coffee break she was free to do what she liked. So she still crept into the room of Monsieur Montrose and read him anything she could get her hands on.

One evening she had an idea. She came in, pulled a chair right up close to the bed, and looked warmly at the middle-aged man lying motionless in drifts of white bed linen. "Pierre," she said cozily, "it's your friend Prudence here. Prudence Lark, your favorite nurse. I saw a wonderful letter in Dear Abby today. Do you want to hear it?"

Pierre Montrose didn't say yes but he didn't say no. So Nurse Lark said, "Dear Abby, I am a nurse at a hospital in Vermont. I have fallen in love with my patient, who is in a deep coma. What should I do? Signed, Worried."

Nurse Lark looked carefully at her beloved Pierre. "Want me to read the answer?" she asked. Pierre Montrose didn't say yes but he didn't say no. So Nurse Lark continued. "Dear Worried: Ever hear of Sleeping Beauty? A good kiss on the lips works wonders. Let me know how it goes."

There was a silence in the room—not unusual. "Shall I try?" asked Nurse Lark. Pierre Montrose didn't say yes but he didn't say no.

Nurse Prudence Lark leaned over and kissed Pierre Montrose.

The door crashed open. Head Nurse Crisp quivered with rage in the doorway. "I heard that! All of it! Unprofessional conduct! You will lose your certification, Nurse Lark!" She marched into the room and snatched up the newspaper. "Look! You've lied! This isn't even Dear Abby, it's the sports section! Nurse Lark, I'm astounded!"

"I'm ashamed!" said Nurse Lark.

"I'm surprised!" said Head Nurse Crisp.

"I'm sorry!" sobbed Nurse Lark.

"I'm hungry," said the patient.

The two nurses spun around. His eyelids fluttered. "Got any hospital Jell-O?" he said in the most enticing French Canadian accent you ever heard; Jell-O sounded like *zhello.* "With no marshmallow, with no spider, with no cherry, *chérie.*"

Head Nurse Crisp was a devoted nurse, no matter how strict a boss she was. She ran for the Jell-O, weeping with joy. She was having a life-changing experience. Nurse Prudence Lark threw her arms around Pierre Montrose. "It worked!" she cried. "Honey! What do you mean, no spiders?"

But Pierre Montrose mumbled, "Some dream, some bad dream," and was too weak to talk much yet. He lay back on the pillows and grinned at his nurse, and whispered, "Read me the part where the heroine saves the hero again." Nurse Lark fumbled for *Love's Tender Torture* in her bag, but her eyes were too filled with tears to read the words.

A hundred miles away, in Foggy Hollow, the four remaining spiders were not so joyful. They were growing bigger. Bigger and angrier. Now *three* of their family had disappeared! And no sign of any of them returning!

Something was changing in the spiders. They felt nasty. The childlike love they harbored for their private goddesses, that special devotion—it was beginning to change. What good had that love done them so far? It had just divided them from one another.

In place of love, a surly sort of vengefulness began to percolate through their veins. They clustered in a throbbing angry knot of poison and mean intentions. The chilling air only hardened their anger.

The senior of the remaining four spiders left around dawn. There was no feeling among them that this spider, either, would return. Well, war was an ugly matter. Stiff upper lip and all that. My spiderweb, right or wrong.

Once more into the breach. It's a far, far better web I spin than I have ever spun.

The warrior tarantula had given up the idea of a love nip. Instead, it wanted to suck blood.

10: Carly's Prize Pumpkin

On both sides of town, hard work was going on.

The Copycats were in the backyard of Sammy Grubb's house, where you could hear the thud of hammers and the occasional mild cuss word. Mr. Grubb had designed a simple web, made on a square wooden frame of two-by-fours and angled supports. The frame would stand six feet high, with a rope web strung from top to bottom but not side to side, as it had to pull apart to allow Hubda the Magnificent to stride through.

Sammy Grubb and Stanislaus wielded the hammers. Hector and Forest Eugene fashioned the web by knotting lengths of ropes and twine together. Mike and Moshe worked on the script. Salim, being the new boy still, hung around on the edges, not sure what to do.

Pearl Hotchkiss, featured guest, practiced making an entrance as Hubda. She was sorry she had agreed to do this—she didn't have the pizzazz and verve of Sharday Wren—but

Sammy seemed to be glad of her help. "I don't even know who Hubda is, really," said Pearl.

"Don't you remember?" said Salim, eager to help. "Miss Earth read to us from the newspaper. She was a tenth-century Siberian woman from a famous poem, *The Epic Verses of Hubda the Magnificent*. Everybody was mentioning her when those snow spiders were discovered in ice last summer. They thought her poem was about mythological beasts. You know, like dragons. But now they wonder if she really was a sort of tenth-century version of Meg Snoople."

"Dragons aren't mythical. They were real," said Stanislaus.

"They were dinosaurs with heartburn," said Hector.

"But that doesn't tell me how Hubda would *walk*," said Pearl crossly. "What she would *do*."

The boys all took turns being Hubda. They demonstrated a catalog of strides, slinks, wobbles, lopes, waddles, goose steps, and limps. Pearl watched seriously and took notes inside her head. She wanted to make a leash for the spider, so she could waltz in with a snappy confidence.

The spider was growing almost daily; it didn't fit in the sandwich bag anymore. It was by now the size of an egg. Pearl kept it in an old terrarium with a heavy lid. It never tried to bite her; it hardly seemed to know she existed.

"But the walk is so brief, backstage to front, what do I do when we get there?" Pearl wailed anxiously.

"We'll make up a poem for you to say," said Sammy. "Not to worry. You're a peach to help us out." He grinned at her. Pearl felt dizzy and looked at her shoes.

Across town, the Tattletales were having a meeting too. They were in Thekla Mustard's gazebo. They were planning "The Haunting of Miss Earth." Anna Maria leaned over the railing uttering her piercing scream in high C until Thekla asked her please to cut it out, *please.* "We are trying to compose a script," she said crossly. "No, Sharday, I *don't* think one of the ghosts should do the tarantella. Lois, stop making faces behind my back. Carly, have you got the pumpkin?"

Carly Garfunkel nodded. "I stopped at the vegetable stand and picked it up yesterday. Last night me and my dad scooped it out and carved a face." She put her arms around the thing and hoisted it up onto the weather-beaten card table. "Look, see? Isn't it scary?"

"You carved it already?" said Thekla, staring at it.

It was scary indeed. Scarier than Carly knew.

Not only did it have a brilliant, snaggletoothed grin and triangular eyes. It also had a presence, a spirit inside it, watching.

For yesterday afternoon the spider, making its way along the path of its siblings, had been poking around the vegetable stand. Sniffing for clues. It had frozen in stunned disbelief when Carly had come along with her wagon. This was the grand magnetic deliciousness it had desired. But it was now in warrior mode, and it squelched its first rush of passion. It became sly. Spreading its eight legs to their widest forcepslike grasp, it hid on the far side of the pumpkin that Carly selected. And it rode to Carly's home with her. In the evening, it skulked behind the stovepipe, coming out only once, in the middle of the night. With delicate movements it slipped in between the jagged orange teeth of the pumpkin's smile. Carly, eagerly carving the pumpkin, had created a hiding place for her own wily spider murderer. Now it looked out of the triangular eye slits and coldly considered its foe.

Carly was saying, "Isn't it creepy?"

"Halloween, and the Pageant, isn't for two weeks," said Thekla slowly. "And by then the edges of this pumpkin will curl and turn brown and go mushy. Corruption in the vegetable kingdom. In a word, Carly: garbage. We don't want our stage set littered with smelly garbage!"

"But isn't it creepy?" said Carly, undisturbed. "I think I did a great job carving it. It looks like—"

"It looks like Thekla Mustard," said Lois. "Well done."

"Lois!" said Thekla. "I don't have to put up with your snotty remarks!"

"Oh, chill out," said Lois, yawning.

"It won't do," said Thekla firmly. "The pumpkin. It'll rot in two weeks. It's a no-go, Carly."

"But this was the biggest pumpkin!" said Carly. "That's why I could do such a great wicked mouth on it!"

"Well, you blew it," said Thekla. "Dump it."

"It'll be fine," Lois said, and when Thekla glared at her, added, "but what do I know?"

"I thought I could rely on you," said Thekla. "Frankly, Carly, you are a letdown."

Carly was crying. Thekla didn't care. The other Tattletales looked away into the woods, embarrassed. "Get rid of it," said Thekla again. "We need a fresh pumpkin for our show, not a two-week-old jack-o'-lantern with toothless gums."

The spider was taking advantage of the heated words. Carly was going to come over and lift up the pumpkin soon. It would leap onto her hand. It would sink its venom into her blood-stream. The girl wouldn't last a minute.

Carly went and picked up the pumpkin. She had half a mind to hurl it at Thekla, but of course she'd never do that. The spider aimed, about to lunge out of the pumpkin's carved mouth.

But just then Anna Maria hit her high C again.

Carly, startled, jumped a few inches and dropped her pumpkin back on the table, where it split into seven pieces.

"I told you to stop that!" snarled Thekla. "We'll practice your part later, Anna Maria!"

But Anna Maria was sobbing and pointing to the table.

Inside the smashed pumpkin was a huge smushed spider.

"It was about to attack Carly!" cried Anna Maria. So the seven Tattletales screamed their *yucks* out for ten minutes. When they had gotten ahold of themselves, they looked more closely.

"I think," said Thekla, "it's the spider that Pearl Hotchkiss brought into class for show-and-tell. The one she said was a Siberian snow spider, though I never for a minute believed *that*. It must have escaped and followed us here."

"Or she trained it to spy on us and report back to her!" suggested Fawn breathlessly.

"Oh Fawn, get a life," they all said together. On the card table, the last nerves of the spider twitched from habit, and were still. With the cold scrutiny of the no-longer-threatened, the girls studied the spider's corpse unflinchingly.

"We'd better not mention this to anyone," said Thekla at last. "We don't want to be accused of spider murder. Poor Pearl. She'll be devastated when she realizes her pet has escaped and has come to a mushy end."

11: Three Spiders Out for Blood

Nurse Lark helped Pierre Montrose into a wheelchair. She wrapped his legs in a blanket. He was recovering—slowly, slowly. Today Nurse Lark had special permission from Head Nurse Crisp to take her patient for a wheel around the grounds. It was a gorgeous day, the last Monday in October, five days before Halloween.

"You have been a very good nurse," said Pierre, holding her hand as they sat on the veranda.

"Thank you. Only my duty," said Nurse Lark, lying a little.

"May I call you Prudence?" said Pierre.

"Yes, you may."

"Prudence," said Pierre, "I live a very simple life. I drive my truck for my company. I stay home weeknights and read Louis L'Amour cowboy books. On Sundays I go to church. I bowl on Saturday nights. Once a year I collect for the Canadian Heart Association. It's a very humble life. I don't even get cable."

"Cable shmable," murmured Prudence Lark, looking into his eyes.

"Soon I will recover, I hope," said Pierre Montrose. "I will be well enough to go back to my little semidetached house in Montreal, with the duck wallpaper and the maple-leaf pattern in the carpet. It will seem very lonely. I will miss your friendly voice."

"And I yours," said Prudence.

"Would you—could you consider—would you—" Pierre Montrose blinked, and blushed, and turned his head for a minute. Then his face whitened. Prudence became Nurse Lark at once. She felt for his pulse.

"Pierre, what's wrong? Speak to me!" she cried.

Pierre Montrose pointed a trembling finger to the edge of the veranda. There, a pretty spiderweb trembled in the October breeze. A few husks of insects, their juices long sucked dry, rotted decoratively here and there and caught the slanting afternoon light like jewels.

"What? What is it?" cried Nurse Lark.

"They're back. They've come to get me," croaked Pierre. "I'm a dead man. Save me, Nurse Lark!"

"*Prudence*," she reminded him. "I've already saved you once. Now what?" Truth to tell, she was faintly annoyed at the interruption of a certain proposal of marriage.

"I just remembered what caused the heart attack!" cried Pierre. "It was a monstrous hairy spider in the cab of my truck. It's coming to get me! I know it is!"

"Nonsense. It's all in your imagination," said Prudence. She stalked to the spiderweb and tore it apart with her hands. "I happen to find spiderwebs beautiful, but there. Does that make you feel better?"

"Marry me, you fearless woman!" roared Pierre.

"I'll consider it," she answered. The thought that her lover might be looney tunes kept her from saying yes right away.

She wheeled the poor trembling man back to his room and turned on the TV. As she was folding up the blanket, she heard the afternoon news.

"This is Meg Snoople," said a silky voice, "reporting from Harvard University in Cambridge, Massachusetts." Prudence Lark and Pierre Montrose both glanced at the TV. "In this exclusive scoop, I ask the questions no one has had the guts to ask. *Where* are the seven Siberian snow spiders? the Arctic tarantulas? Where, where, Professor Williams, where?" She turned and thrust the microphone at a white-haired scientist coming out of a shoe repair store. "Where are they?"

The scientist mumbled, "Very improper, very

improper," and hid himself behind a pair of old scuffed brogans with new heels.

Meg Snoople advanced toward the cameraman, her perfect face a huge blossom of indignation, right out to the edges of the screen. "America is in a tizzy!" she said. "America has the right to know! The spiders were photographed in a block of ice, being loaded on a truck in Montreal. But did the shipment ever arrive at Harvard? What happened to it? Stay tuned as Meg Snoople follows this trail of corruption, complicity, and coverup! *Spidergate* continues tomorrow! Tune in!"

Nurse Lark had come across the room, and now she sat on the edge of Pierre Montrose's bed. "Oh, Pierre," she said. "I'm sorry I snapped at you. Now I understand. Was *that* your cargo?"

"They didn't tell me," said Pierre Montrose, "but my instructions were to go to the science labs at Harvard." He shuddered again. She kissed him.

The door flung open. Head Nurse Crisp stood framed in the doorway. "Nurse Lark! You're at it again! For shame!"

"We're engaged to be married, Head Nurse Crisp," said Nurse Lark.

"Well," Head Nurse Crisp snorted, flummoxed, "all I can say to that is: CONGRATU-

LATIONS!" She burst into tears and fled toward a box of Kleenex at the nurses' station. She loved a happy ending as much as anyone else, even if she was a battleaxe.

"She's a weird item," said Pierre, kissing his fiancée.

"She's a good head nurse and a good boss," said Prudence, kissing her fiancé.

A few hours later, in Foggy Hollow, the three remaining tarantulas dined on the corpse of a young squirrel they had managed to trap in their web. The blood of the squirrel was nourishing. The spiders were stronger, faster, and more alert than their siblings had been.

And they were angrier.

Each one of the three had a mental picture of evil. It had been their picture of perfection, but as the weeks went on their attitudes were changing. They had no way of sharing their personal visions of the enemy, of course. In one spider it was Thekla Mustard. For another it was Fawn Petros. And for the youngest spider it was Lois Kennedy the Third. But they shared a thirst for blood.

The spiders knew that their siblings had left, not to return. Now they had a different campaign plan in mind. They *wouldn't* split up. That was only suicide. They would work together.

At dawn, the three spiders, like three muske-teers, set off in single file, following the trail of their departed siblings, determined not to make the same mistakes. Their stomachs rum-bled and their mouths watered for blood. Human blood. Tattletale blood.

12: Thekla Spells *Tarantula*

Thekla Mustard was annoyed. Yesterday she had tried to rehearse the Tattletales in their Halloween pageant skit, which would be on Friday—and today was already Tuesday! The Tattletales needed a strict leader. They chewed gum, they didn't listen. Only Anna Maria, secure in her high C, was doing her part of the haunted Miss Earth with gusto. The others were lackluster. Thekla tried to think of how to make them improve.

"Are you paying attention, Thekla?" It was the voice of the real Miss Earth, cutting through Thekla's thoughts. Thekla blushed. She prided herself on being a model student. And worrying about the skit had made her mind wander!

"Of *course* I was paying attention, Miss Earth," said Thekla hotly. But she didn't have any idea what Miss Earth had been talking about.

"Well, would you care to comment?"

Thekla stood up. In cases such as this it was possible, just possible, to brazen it out. "I would propose that we stand back from the matter at hand," said Thekla pertly, "and consider it in its wider context. What is the basic dilemma here? Are the terms of reference valid? Responsible students, it seems to me, must ask these questions *first.*"

The class began to howl with laughter.

"Am I to take it that no, you *haven't* lost your bus pass?" said Miss Earth. She winked at Thekla. "I'll send a note to the secretary then that the missing bus pass found on the playground this morning wasn't from anyone in our room."

Thekla sat down. She wasn't used to losing dignity like this. She folded her hands on her desk and stared straight ahead.

"Haw haw haw haw!" The class sounded like a flock of asthmatic crows.

By and by the hubbub died down. Miss Earth suggested a spelling bee. The students begged to be allowed to go girls against boys, but that was too much like Copycats and Tattletales, of which Miss Earth disapproved. She divided the class alphabetically. Salim Bannerjee to Lois Kennedy the Third—A to K—was one side, and the other included Anna Maria Mastrangelo to Sharday Wren—M to W. The M to W team had eight members, so they had to go first.

"This will be a Current Events spelling bee," said Miss Earth, perching herself on a wooden stool in the center of the room. "I've taken words from the newspapers today. Remember: say the word, spell it, say it again. Ready? All right. Anna Maria Mastrangelo." Miss Earth grinned. "A word you got wrong on last week's quiz. Poison."

"P—" began Anna Maria.

"Say it spell it say it!" the class screeched.

"Poison," said Anna Maria. "P-O-Y-S-A-N. Poison. Am I right?"

"What kind of a poysan does ya take me for?" said Miss Earth wittily, and rang her little bell, which meant: Sit down.

Anna Maria flopped down in her seat. She was so ashamed to be the first person out. She squeezed her eyes shut and listened to Salim Bannerjee spell it right. P-O-I-S-O-N. Because her eyes were shut, she didn't see three tarantulas climb in through the open window and hide behind the hamster cage. (Later, they found the hamsters, both Bert *and* Ernie, dead of heart attacks. No one could guess why.)

"Spiderweb," said Miss Earth to Forest Eugene Mopp.

"Spiderweb. S-P-I-D-E-R-W-E-B," said Forest Eugene.

Miss Earth made a little encouraging move in the air with her hand.

"Spiderweb," he said again.

The spiders inched along the broad windowsill. They crouched behind the sixteen class paperback copies of *Charlotte's Web*, which were yellowing from the sunlight and looking rumpled from so many affectionate readings.

"Tarantula," said Miss Earth.

"T-A-R-A-N-A-T-A-T-A-T-A . . ." began Nina Bueno.

Bing went the bell. Nina sat down. The A to K team was now losing—they had six members still standing; the M to Ws had seven.

Thekla Mustard was next. She said crisply, "Tarantula. T-A-R-A-N-T-U-L-A. Tarantula."

The three spiders peered through a triangular space where two books leaned against each other. The lead spider saw in Thekla Mustard the source of its wild longing, which once had been love and now was murder. The other two spiders had to squash down their own feelings. The boss spider was now alpha spider, and they were but as minions to its whims.

The boss spider went slowly, one spinneret at a time, along the windowsill, behind the geraniums. The other two followed it.

"Iceland," said Miss Earth to Moshe Cohn.

"That's easy." He spelled it correctly.

The spiders made it to the Quiet Corner without being seen. They dropped on threads to the afghan that Miss Earth sometimes wrapped herself in when she read to the class from the rocking chair. They hid in it, among its zany patterned squares and bright stitchings.

Miss Earth said to Fawn Petros, "Glacier."

No one was more surprised than Fawn that she got it right.

The spiders looked at Thekla Mustard. She stood against the blackboard, about twelve feet away. If they could climb to the chalk tray, they could skitter along that. Thekla Mustard had her hands folded behind her back. Working together now, they could take three little nips in her knuckles. She'd be dead in a matter of minutes. The spiders didn't *know* this, of course. But they *hoped* it. Each creature has a defense system against predators, and in spiders it is—sometimes—their bite.

"Antidote," said Miss Earth to Carly Garfunkel.

"What's *that?*" she said, playing for time.

"It's the substance used to counteract poison," said Miss Earth.

"Antidote," sighed Carly. "A-U-N-T-I-E-D-O-U-B-T. Antidote."

Bing went the bell. Carly sat down. So did Mike Saint Michael. But Sammy Grubb got it right.

The three spiders had decided on their plan of attack. A computer on a rolling stand stood near the blackboard. They could scurry up the thick black power cord and make a little leap onto the chalk tray. Since all eyes in the room were swiveling toward whoever was spelling, they had to stay very still whenever people looked their way. But the spelling bee moved fast. Stanislaus Tomaski was *bing*ed to his seat after misspelling *catastrophe*. Now it was Lois Kennedy the Third's turn.

"Cata—cata— I can't even *say* it," complained Lois.

"Ca-*tas*-tro-phe," said Miss Earth patiently. The three spiders scrabbled up the power cord.

"Catastrophe," said Lois. "C-A-T. That's all I can spell. D-O-G." She sat down in a flump of anger at the whole stupid *idea* of spelling.

Attention swiveled back to the M to W team by the blackboard. The three spiders froze in the tray.

"C-A-T-A-S-T-R-O-P-H-E," said Hector Yellow. Miss Earth looked at him with her eyes bugging out. "*What?*" he said.

"Say it spell it say it," the class roared.

"Oh, catastrophe," he rattled, "K-A-T-O-S-T-R-I-F-E-E. Catastrophe."

"You got it right the first time," said Miss Earth. "I'll give it to you."

"Cheat! Foul! No fair!" everyone yelled, more out of habit than conviction. Miss Earth's decision was law and they knew it.

The teacher turned to Pearl Hotchkiss and said, "Trauma."

"Trauma. T-R-A-U-M-A. Trauma." Pearl bounced against the map of the world in pleasure at such an easy word.

"Now, Sharday," said Miss Earth, "a special word for you. Tarantella."

"The dance, my dance." Sharday grinned. "Tarantella. T-A-R . . ." She paused to think.

The spiders scooted behind her. They couldn't move till she was done.

". . . A-N-T-E-L-L-A!" she finished proudly.

"End of the first round!" said Miss Earth. "And the score is, let's see, A to K team, four players left, and M to W team, five players left. But the M to W team had one more player, so it's really a draw. Shall we keep on?"

"Yes!" yelled everyone. The spiders raced along the tray behind Hector Yellow. Thekla Mustard stood only a foot away now, right next to Fawn.

"Miss Earth?" It was the intercom. "This is Mrs. Cobble."

"Yes, Mrs. Cobble," called Miss Earth to the school secretary in fluting tones.

"May I see Thekla Mustard about a bus pass found in the schoolyard this morning? We think it's hers."

"Yes, Mrs. Cobble." Miss Earth gave a shrug. "I guess that's a good place to end our spelling bee. So, Thekla, you *did* lose your bus pass. Well, hurry along. Class, be seated."

Everyone laughed at Thekla for having lost her bus pass and not even knowing it. She definitely did *not* like people laughing at her! She hurried away. But she didn't know that her demon spider, the boss spider of the day, had just managed to attach a thread to the cuff of her sleeve as she moved away from the chalk tray. When she flounced out the door, the spider was dragged along a foot or two behind. Thekla slammed the door in her rage, and the spider was caught just exactly in the pounding of the door into its jamb.

The other two spiders retreated behind the computer, to think about what to do now that they were the only two left.

13: Two Spiders Biding Their Time

The two tarantulas spent most of Tuesday behind the computer. When Forest Eugene Mopp went to work on it in the afternoon, they shivered with annoyance and fear. But they didn't attack him. They could feel the danger of being the only two left.

They didn't know, of course, what had happened to the first four others. But they did know that the fifth had been squished in the doorway. They could see its gunky remains dribbling down the doorpost. After the school bell sounded and the children all ran screaming home, the spiders watched the janitor come along with a bucket of sudsy water and clean the spider's corpse away. "Oh, the little tykes with their spitballs!" said Mr. Stripe, rinsing his rags and moving on.

The spiders spent the evening exploring Miss Earth's classroom. They clambered inside desks and zigzagged across bulletin boards. They sat on Miss Earth's little bell, which had a push button on top, and they took turns making it ring in the moonlight. They weren't in any hurry anymore. Now they knew that this was the meeting place of their dreaded enemies, they could afford to go slowly.

By the time the sun came up on Wednesday, the two spiders had found a perfect hiding place. They had spun a web between the screen used for movies and the wall behind it. It was dark and dusty back there, so they knew the screen wasn't often moved.

When Miss Earth arrived at 7:30, she didn't know they were there. She took off her motorcycle goggles first, and soon discovered the poor hamsters dead in their cage and removed them. Then she sat down with a cup of tea in a mug that said "For Our Teacher from Your Little Monsters," with a drawing of monster kids on it, and ate her banana-cream doughnut. She flapped open the local newspaper, *The Hamlet Times*. At the bottom of page two there was a little item that Miss Earth found interesting.

MEG SNOOPLE DISCOVERS RARE SPIDERS ARE MISSING!

Miss Earth clipped the five-line article to read aloud during Current Events period. By the time her first student arrived, she had brushed the sugar dust off her lips and was standing, pert and smiling and ready to lead the new generation toward a glorious future, as usual.

A hundred miles away or so, the breakfast reading of Pierre Montrose and Prudence Lark also included an article on Meg Snoople. "So now they're admitting it in public," said Nurse Lark. "The spiders never arrived at Harvard! And you know what happened to them, don't you, Pierre?"

He nodded grimly over his breakfast mush.

"Do you think you have an obligation to tell someone?" said Nurse Lark. "After all, someone might be bitten by one. Who knows what venom pulses through those defrosted spider veins?"

"Exactly so," said Pierre. "I wonder how I could get Meg Snoople on the phone."

Just then Head Nurse Crisp burst in. She had taken to listening in at the keyhole for most of her working day (well, it was so rewarding, you learned so *much*). She didn't even bother to pretend she was dusting the keyhole, the way she usually did when found out. She merely said, "Well, of course, ninnies, call ABC! Call CBS! What station does Snoople work for? Call NBC! Call CNN! Call the FBI! Call the CIA!"

"Well, I suppose," said Nurse Lark and Pierre Montrose.

"Call Scotland Yard! Call Interpol! Call the Kremlin! Call NATO! Call the United Nations! Call 'The Undersea World of Jacques Cousteau'!"

"But spiders don't live underwater," said Nurse Lark, confused.

"These are dangerous beasts, no sense taking chances!" yelled Head Nurse Crisp. She yanked Pierre Montrose out of bed, revealing his behind, which flashed out of the hospital gown, and plopped him in a wheelchair. She and Nurse Lark raced him down the hall and nearly killed him crashing into the nurses' station. With trembling fingers he dialed Directory Assistance.

"The number I need is for Snoople," he said to the operator. "Meg Snoople."

At two o'clock that Wednesday afternoon, a helicopter came down out of the sky, droning like a cicada, and landed on the lawn in front of the cafeteria. Local TV cameras were on hand to catch pictures of Meg Snoople, showing an awful lot of shapely leg, getting out of the helicopter while the blades were still making hurricane winds. Why she didn't just wait till the blades came to rest wasn't clear to Nurse Lark. But her hair did blow across her face in a pretty dramatic, movie star–like way.

Meg Snoople ran across the lawn with a microphone in her hand, like a lion tamer with a piece of meat on a fork. She poked the microphone into the face of the first person she saw and said, "The mystery is no longer in your hands, Miss—Miss—" She tried to read the name tag on the nurse who was standing in front of her with folded arms across her starched bosom.

"Head Nurse Crisp," said Head Nurse Crisp. "Follow me, Meg Snoople, for the scoop of your career."

Head Nurse Crisp stalked down the corridor, which had been specially waxed at lunchtime so it would look good on national TV. In a short skirt wrapped tightly around her thighs, Meg Snoople could hardly keep up with her. "In here, our recovering patient Pierre Montrose," Head Nurse Crisp said, pushing open a door with a snappy flourish of her hand.

Meg Snoople thrust the microphone at the man in the bed.

"What do you know about the spiders?" she asked.

"I believe I was carrying them from Montreal to Boston," he told her. "I saw one in my cab. I crashed my truck up. They may have been killed in the crash. Or maybe they escaped."

"Where was this?" screamed Meg Snoople. "America demands the truth!"

"Hang on to your teeth, I'm going to tell you," said Pierre Montrose. "I invited *you* here, lady, remember?"

"Cut that part out," said Meg to the cameraman. "And: film. Where was this? America demands the truth!"

"You already said that," said Pierre Montrose.

"Cut," said Meg Snoople. "Look," she said in a quieter voice. "It's been a long day. I got a job to do. You got a job to do. We all got a job to do. This is my job. Let me do my job? Please?"

"But of course," said Pierre Montrose gallantly.

"Thank you," said Meg Snoople. "Nothing personal, of course. Ready with the camera? And: *film*. Where was this? America demands to know!"

"You know, I don't like people talking to me in that tone of voice," said Pierre Montrose. "I'm from Canada, where folks are polite."

"I'm going to go crazy unless you tell me!" shrieked Meg Snoople.

"Hamlet, Vermont," said Pierre Montrose, winking at the camera, and then he said to the cameraman, "That's a wrap, fella."

Pierre Montrose had wasted so much of Meg

Snoople's time that she couldn't get to Hamlet, Vermont, that afternoon. She decided to go back to Boston and try again the next day. After reviewing the tape, she chose not to use it, because Pierre Montrose had been so unhelpful. She would hold the story back for twenty-four hours. It wasn't as if she was endangering the public, was it? How much better a news story it would make if she could land in the middle of the town square of Hamlet, Vermont, and broadcast the terrifying report with a bullhorn on live evening news!

So she took her helicopter back to Logan Airport in Boston, and slept the sleep of the just at the Park Plaza.

The next day she had her hair done and shopped on Newbury Street for a smart new outfit. She couldn't let the lid off this one until 6:00 P.M., when it could make the evening news all up and down the East Coast. So she dilly-dallied, even taking a ride in a swan boat on Boston Common.

While Meg Snoople dilly-dallied, Pearl Hotchkiss was showing Sammy Grubb how to make plastic spiders in the Spider Fun Factory. Pearl had been invited over to Sammy's house, since it was Pearl's dad who worked for the toy company and had gotten the Spider Fun Factory for free. Pearl and Sammy had a nice afternoon filling the mold with colored gloop. After some experimentation they got it down pretty well. They figured out how to expand the mold, using bent paper clips, to make even larger and more flexible spiders. They laughed a lot, and Pearl got over being shy with Sammy. It was fun.

In the classroom, the two spiders hadn't budged from behind their screen all day. They knew they hadn't many chances to take their revenge. They could come forward only when they had the perfect opportunity.

14: Fawn Bobs for Apples

Halloween was coming up on Friday. The Josiah Fawcett Elementary School Halloween Pageant of Horrors would be held at an assembly in the auditorium on Friday afternoon. This was only Wednesday, but Miss Earth's classroom was already decorated with cardboard cutouts of skulls, craggy-faced green witches, and ghosts. At noon the lunch lady, Mrs. Brill, was planning her own little early Halloween surprise for the children in Miss Earth's class—early because Mrs. Brill had anther job on Thursdays and Fridays and couldn't do it then.

Mrs. Brill arrived around eleven o'clock Wednesday morning. Making a number of trips, she carried in from the trunk of her car a green plastic basin, a sack of McIntosh apples, a tray of cookies shaped like poisonous mushrooms and iced with yummy-yucky green fake-poison frosting, and paper napkins with red and orange leaves on them. She also brought a pumpkin, some gourds, paper cups with red and orange leaves on them, and apple cider in plastic jugs. She lugged in a papier-mâché skull, painted black and white, with candy inside. She had a large painting of a hissing black cat rolled up under one arm. She dumped all this stuff in the back of the classroom.

The room was dark because the shades were drawn. As a pre-Halloween treat, Miss Earth was showing a movie, *The Wizard of Oz*. The most deliciously bad witch of all time, the Wicked Witch of the West, cackled in her famous fiendish way. "I'll get *you* and your little dog too!" she screeched. Behind the screen, the two tarantulas twitched their legs in fellow feeling.

When the movie ended and the fluorescent lights came on, Miss Earth and Mrs. Brill were both found to be blowing their noses in the napkins. "What's wrong?" said Sammy Grubb.

"There *is* no place like home, just as they say in the movie," whispered Miss Earth to her class.

Mrs. Brill nodded solemnly. "When you're older you'll learn."

"There's no place like *school*," said Sammy loyally, and all the children shouted "HUR-RAY!" There *was* no place like school, especially on a day with a movie and a lunchtime party.

They whipped through some higher math, and then the lunch bell rang. Miss Earth took herself off to the teachers' lounge for her low-fat cottage cheese, her celery sticks, and her raspberry-mousse doughnut. Mrs. Brill made the children eat their lunches before they had the party games.

"We'll play pin the tail on the witch's cat, then we'll have a skull piñata, then we'll bob for apples," said Mrs. Brill. The kids chomped through their lunches as quickly as possible.

The two spiders weren't planning an attack that day. Each one had its own target, of course. The slightly larger one was after Fawn Petros, and the smaller one was hooked on Lois Kennedy the Third. The spiders had climbed out of their web to the top of the movie screen during *The Wizard of Oz* and peered at the glaring light of the projector, but all they had been able to make out were silhouettes. So they had scuttled back, to wait for the right moment.

"Pin the tail on the witch's cat. I stayed up all night painting this thing," said Mrs. Brill proudly. With masking tape she fixed the huge picture to the movie screen.

It didn't look much like a cat, the kids thought; it looked like the bag of dust taken from the inside of a vacuum cleaner, except with legs and some huge boiled-egg eyes, and minus, of course, a tail. But they were too polite to say anything except "Purr, purr."

They drew lots to see who would go first.

Mike St. Michael won. Mrs. Brill fixed the bandanna around his eyes, checked to make sure he couldn't cheat on purpose or by accident, and handed him the tail of the witch's cat. It was a strip of paper painted black, and one end had a sharp dressmaker's pin stuck through it. "Now the rule is that if you come near a person, we'll steer you away so you don't accidentally jab anyone," said Mrs. Brill. "And wherever you first touch we'll mark with masking tape and write your initials on it. The person who gets nearest to the rump of the witch's cat, wins."

She spun Mike St. Michael around. He wasn't good about getting dizzy and fell on the floor almost at once. When he got up he touched the tail to the hamster cage (which was now draped in a black cloth, with notes of sorrow and grief attached with tape to the front). "Gee, that's hard," he said.

Nobody did very well. Mrs. Brill was an excellent spinner. Carly Garfunkel went out the open classroom door and pinned the wall in the hall. Hector Yellow tagged Miss Earth's coat hanging on a peg. Nina Bueno touched the movie projector, and Salim Bannerjee blundered against the computer. Thekla Mustard nearly got Mrs. Brill herself, but she was steered away and landed at the geraniums on the windowsill. Moshe Cohn came very close, almost to the screen, but at the last minute turned and selected his own desk instead. Then it was Fawn Petros's turn.

"I can see," she kept whining. "Make it tighter."

Mrs. Brill retied the bandanna several times, twirled Fawn, and said, "There ye be."

Fawn tilted back and forth a bit until the dark in her mind stopped spinning, and then began a cautious movement here, there, this way, that.

Sammy Grubb was standing on a chair trying to hang up the skull piñata for the next game, and Fawn almost jabbed his bum. "Look out, Sammy!" cried Pearl. Sammy jumped to safety just in time, and cast a grateful glance at Pearl, which melted her heart away. Fawn then turned and weaved her way toward the back of the room. The kids became silent as she got nearer and nearer to the movie screen.

With a sudden decisive punch Fawn reached out and drove the tail, with its sharp pin, right into the painting of the cat, very near its rear end. Right through the paper, right through the screen, into the web behind the screen.

The spiders were startled but not hurt. They darted away from the lethal weapon, which tore a hole in an essential part of their web. From the top of their home, now falling in shreds, they watched the pin wiggle and wag.

The senior of the two spiders peeked over

the top of the screen. He saw, and recognized, Fawn Petros, whipping off the bandanna and laughing in pleasure at her good aim.

The younger spider began immediately to repair the damaged web. The senior spider took advantage of the fun below to scurry across the ceiling. It hadn't intended to attack Fawn Petros just then, but if *she* was going to attack first, it certainly intended to defend itself. The spider slid down the string to the top of the papier-mâché skull. This was a good vantage point. The skull was large, and the spider could flatten itself against the top and be invisible to the human monsters below. Maybe it could leap on top of Fawn Petros and chew her head off.

From its lookout the spider watched as the rest of the class played pin the tail on the witch's cat. No one came anywhere near as close as Fawn Petros, so she was declared the winner. And her prize? She got to be the first one to take a whack at the piñata.

Mrs. Brill put the same bandanna around Fawn's eyes and gave her the yardstick. She twirled Fawn around again and motioned the other students to back off. "Away ye go," cried Mrs. Brill.

Fawn Petros made a few probing feints with the yardstick. Then with the accuracy of a

World Series batter she aimed straight at the piñata and gave it a mighty whack. The spider couldn't believe the bloodthirstiness of its foe. A spray of wrapped candies and bits of skull fell through the air. What also fell, although in the melee no one noticed it, was the spider. It was knocked from its perch and it plopped in the tub of water, into which Mrs. Brill had just dumped fifteen juicy greenish-red apples.

The children scrambled for candy prizes and everyone had found at least something. "I should have made the piñata stronger," said Mrs. Brill. "Next year I'll use quick-drying cement. Now let's draw straws again to see who gets to bob for apples first."

There was no prize for bobbing for apples, just the fun and slop of getting wet. Sharday Wren won the draw, and Mrs. Brill wrapped her in a smock to protect her clothes. As the other students looked on, Sharday locked her hands behind her back and thrust her face toward the apples jostling in the water. She chased them around, and finally with a huge bite caught a big juicy apple and raised it, dripping, with her teeth.

And the spider? It kept taking deep breaths and plunging underwater, trying to keep on the bottom side of the floating apples. This spider was canny underwater.

Stanislaus Tomaski went next, and then Sammy Grubb, and then Pearl Hotchkiss, and then Forest Eugene Mopp. Anna Maria Mastrangelo didn't want to because she didn't like getting her face wet. Lois Kennedy the Third felt sick from eating everyone else's apples. Soon it was time for Fawn Petros.

But not many kids were watching at this point. They were all annoyed at Fawn for winning *both* games, and suspected that despite her loud remarks she *had* been able to see out of the corner of the bandanna. So only Mrs. Brill was standing by, with a huge smile on her face, to make sure Fawn didn't accidentally drown herself in the tub of water.

There were four apples left, and the spider, below water level, kept moving quickly from one to another, like an athletic barnacle beneath a ship.

Fawn wasn't very good at this game, since it wasn't possible to cheat at it. Her very first move was to plunge her face three inches deep into the water. The spider studied her face at close range. It was now or never!

Fawn bobbed again. The spider lunged, but missed. Several times Fawn's face appeared, and several times the spider pushed off toward her, but always she pulled out too quickly.

And then it happened. Fawn caught an apple!

She lifted it with her teeth and held it triumphantly for all to see. Making a wordless crow, she made her classmates turn and look at her.

With a single voice they screamed: "Spider!"

It had come dripping out of the water on the back side of Fawn's apple. Now it crawled around to the top, an inch from Fawn's eyes, which were crossing in the effort to bring it into focus.

Whack!

The apple was gone. The spider was gone. There was a fruity splat against the wall. Mrs. Brill had whipped her yardstick with unerring accuracy, straight at the apple. A small, delicate, bite-sized piece of apple, the only part left, fell out of Fawn's mouth.

15: One Spider Plans Revenge

As Miss Earth studied the creepy corpse of the tarantula on the wall, she wondered for a minute if authorities should be called in. "I've lived in Vermont all my life, and I've never seen such a creature before," she murmured. "Pearl, is this the spider you brought in for show-and-tell in September?"

"Nah," said Pearl. "That's at home. We keep it in the old terrarium. We feed it pepperoni pizza, but we don't get too close."

Thekla Mustard elbowed her way past Mrs. Brill. "Does this remind the Tattletales of anything?" she said. They all nodded. *"Exactly,"* snapped Thekla. "The gross spider squished by Carly's pumpkin. We thought *it* was Pearl's spider."

"Wasn't *my* spider," said Pearl.

"Well, I do wonder," said Miss Earth. "I'm sorry the poor creature had to die, but of course, Mrs. Brill, you did the right thing, not knowing whether it was dangerous. Oh, don't clean it up!" But Mrs. Brill had already swabbed at the mess on the wall with a paper towel seasonally decorated with red and orange leaves.

Miss Earth resolved to pick up the *New York Times* and the *Boston Globe* on her way home from school that day to see if anything more was revealed on the missing Siberian snow spiders. She strongly doubted this could be one of them, but then, what about the other spider the girls said had been squished by a pumpkin? And the one Pearl had caught? Surely the authorities would have alerted a public in danger of spider bites! Something unusual was going on. But it wasn't right to cause a panic.

"Clean up your party mess," said Miss Earth, clapping her hands. "We'll spend the next hour in the auditorium practicing our skits."

The children all applauded Mrs. Brill for a wonderful lunchtime Halloween party. They agreed that the yucky spider had made a perfect touch of horror. Then they single-filed down the hall to the auditorium, where the kindergartners, dressed up as mice, were just finishing their Halloween skit. (Kindergartners were always mice in the Christmas pageant too; it saved on costumes and they were good at it.)

"Miss Earth's class!" boomed Mrs. Cobble, the school secretary, who was in charge of rehearsals. She peered at a clipboard in her hand. "I see your ten-minute slot is divided into two separate skits. Well, skit one get ready, and let's have a walk-through. On the double."

The Tattletales were going first. They giggled a lot and made Miss Earth leave the auditorium because they wanted their skit to be a surprise. Miss Earth took this chance to go turn on the afternoon news on the radio to listen for anything about the missing spiders.

Thekla had worked out the staging ahead of time. With a snap of her fingers she ordered the Tattletales to drag six school desks from the wings. She herself pulled out a rolling blackboard, on which she wrote in huge letters that could be seen clear to the back of the room

MISS EARTH'S CLASSROOM,
ON HALLOWEEN.

"Places, and *action!*" yelled Mrs. Cobble through a megaphone made of rolled-up cardboard. She dropped the needle of the school record player on the album called *Creepy Music to Scare Your Socks Off*. It sounded a bit scratchy, but still the music gave a wonderful sense of mysterious danger.

On walked Anna Maria dressed as Miss Earth, in high heels and motorcycle goggles, with a pocketbook, a newspaper, a pile of paperbacks, and a small white paper sack. She sat down on the edge of the card table they were pretending was her desk, opened up the sack, and took out a real jelly doughnut. She ate it, looking this way and that as the music got creepier. Everyone was howling with laughter because Anna Maria did a good job. Then she tapped Miss Earth's little bell and said loudly, "I wonder where my dear students could be today?"

That was the cue for the other Tattletales to come drifting onto the stage, dressed in old bedsheets with eyeholes cut in them. They "woohed" and "waaahed" and waved their arms about. Anna Maria/Miss Earth pretended not to see them and said broadly to the audience, "I wonder what that strange noise is?" Finally they danced right up to her and touched her with their spooky sheets, and Anna Maria pulled her legs up underneath her, threw her head back, whipped off the goggles, and let it rip, that famous high C.

"Aaaaaaaaaaaaaaaaaaaaaaaaaaaaaaaaaaaaaaaa aaaaaaaaaaaaaaahhhhhhhhh!!!"

The ghosts fell back. "Who're YOU?" asked the mock Miss Earth. Offstage Mrs. Cobble lifted the needle off the record.

To the tune of "She'll Be Comin' Round the Mountain When She Comes," the ghosts sang,

> *We're the ghosts of former students, dear*
>   *Miss Earth!*
>   *Dear Miss Earth!*
> *And we realize what your teaching skills*
>   *are worth,*
>   *Dear Miss Earth!*
> *So we've come back not to haunt you,*
> *Not to tease you or to taunt you,*
> *But to thank you for your wisdom and*
>   *your mirth,*
>   *Dear Miss Earth!*

Then, in a move that the waiting Copycats and Pearl Hotchkiss thought was a little over the top, Anna Maria/Miss Earth and her ghost-students all linked arms and did a high-kick step, just as they had done the year before when they were all Frankenstein's brides, and sang,

> *She'll be teaching lucky students every*
>   *year,*
>   *every year,*
> *She'll be teaching lucky students every*
>   *year,*
>   *every year,*
> *You can be a lucky student*

If you're plucky and you're prudent,
She'll be teaching lucky students every
  year,
      give a cheer!

Mrs. Cobble advised strongly that they end the skit right there and not go into "For She's a Jolly Good Teacher," to the tune of which they had intended to do a conga line off the stage. "Very lovely I'm sure," bawled Mrs. Cobble. "Hurry offstage now, the boys next. Keep this moving, we've got four hundred kids to get on and off the stage in fifty-five minutes, no time for shilly-shallying."

The stage manager, a high school kid, brought the lights down as the girls tugged their props offstage and the boys dragged theirs on. The huge wooden frame knotted with rope to look like a six-foot-tall spiderweb looked eerie and grim in the dim light. Mrs. Cobble yelled, "Ready? And: music!" and she dropped the needle of the record player down in the appropriate groove. It bounced a little scratchily and settled into the slow, sinuous theme music suggesting spiders, poison, and death.

The Tattletales stood watching. The seven Copycats had all changed into black jeans and T-shirts or black track suits. Like a team of underground guerrilla fighters they swarmed onto the stage, crouched down and moving as much like spiders as they could.

Then the lights went lower and Hector and Moshe pulled apart the two sides of the web. Pearl Hotchkiss strode through, dressed all in black, with a hood over her head. Mrs. Cobble jerked the needle out of the record, and the boys began to drone, more a low-voiced chant than an actual melody, these words:

> *Spiderwebs can catch at you, catch at you,*
>   *catch at you.*
> *Spiderwebs can snatch at you, my fair*
>   *Hubda.*
> *Poison spiders cling to you, sing to you,*
>   *cling to you,*
> *Spiders may we bring to you, my fair*
>   *Hubda.*

Here the boys all drew from under their sweatshirts or T-shirts the plastic spiders that Sammy Grubb and Pearl Hotchkiss had made. The things were huge, and their lengthy legs were stiffened with paper clips; they flopped on the floor and quivered around Pearl "Hubda" Hotchkiss, who struck an exotic pose of power and said in a carrying tone:

> *Little Miss Muffet sat on a tuffet,*

Eating her curds and whey,
Along came a spider who sat down beside
  her—
Miss Muffet gets buried today.

The boys had tied elastic thread to the limbs of the plastic spiders, and twitched the lines so it looked as if the spiders were dancing up and down to the final verse that the boys chanted:

If a spider bites your throat, please take
  note, don't you gloat;
No one has an antidote, my fair Hubda.

Everyone in the auditorium screamed with gratifying noise at the seven twitching spiders. The Tattletales were dismayed. It looked as if the Copycats had had a better skit idea after all. "Perhaps we should have a new Empress of the Tattletales?" Lois Kennedy the Third hissed in the direction of Thekla when dress rehearsal was over.

Behind the movie screen, the last free spider was still quivering with shock and rage at the untimely death of its sibling. It almost didn't notice the quivering rubbery spiders the boys kept bouncing on their strings like yoyos.

Almost. But then it did.

And it began to plan its own little skit for the Halloween Pageant of Horrors at the Josiah Fawcett Elementary School.

16: Lois Marked for Murder

On Thursday morning when Pierre Montrose woke up, the doctors pronounced him well enough to leave. They bundled him up in clean clothes and gave him a little paper sack of tissues and aspirin and a complimentary thermometer as a souvenir. Head Nurse Crisp was waiting on the steps with a bunch of roses for Nurse Prudence Lark and Pierre Montrose when they appeared, Nurse Lark pushing the wheelchair. She was taking a week's holiday to go to Montreal to have a good look around before deciding to settle down there.

"We'll miss you," said Head Nurse Crisp, bravely holding back her tears as she hugged Prudence and shook Pierre's hand. "You've brought life back to this old place, real human life. I do love life, when I remember to think about it. So refreshing, really."

"I don't know what to say but thanks," said Pierre.

"We're going to make a detour down to Hamlet before we head for Montreal,"

Prudence Lark said as she settled into the driver's seat of her little red Fiat. "Meg Snoople never aired her interview with Pierre yesterday, and we think she might try to do something splashier from Hamlet."

"I have an uncontrollable urge to see the scene of my crash," admitted Pierre. "If the spiders really are on the loose, I would like to know about it, even though it gives me the creeps."

"Well, why didn't you say so?" said Head Nurse Crisp. She yanked open the back door of the car and plopped herself in among the suitcases. "There might be mass trauma and panic if that Meg Snoople alarms everyone! It's my duty to public health that I make myself available in such a crisis! Nurse Lark, drive on; I'll phone in at the first gas station to tell people at the hospital I'm off for a day or two." And out of the driveway the red Fiat sped, heading for Interstate 89.

Nurse Lark and Pierre Montrose were right, for even then Meg Snoople was making her plans for a doozy of a live broadcast. She had her chauffeur drive her limousine into Hamlet and park it behind the Grand Union supermarket, and in dark glasses and a trench coat Meg Snoople went wandering about the small town center. She liked what she saw. Hamlet was a pretty town, with a classic New England wooden church painted white, and a village green in the center, and some low brick buildings that looked quaint and olden-timey and had shutters and chrysanthemums and signs like "Hamlet Country Store" and things like cheddar cheese, maple syrup, and apple cider in the windows. Meg Snoople wondered if she could import a couple of cows to graze on the green. She called Boston to see if they had any cows in the prop department, but Boston said no, try to get some locally. But that would be giving away her hand, so Meg Snoople decided against the cows. Besides, what if the helicopter accidentally landed on them? That wouldn't make the kind of news she wanted.

The cameraman would arrive in time for the six o'clock broadcast and set up the lights. She would come down in her helicopter, interview the first person she saw, tell him or her about the spiders maybe being on the loose, and get the person's horrified reaction. This would be at ten after six in the evening, right during the rush hour, so there'd be sure to be tons of people around. She'd go from citizen to citizen, stirring things up, and finish by rushing up to the church steps, maybe, and jabbing a proclamation marked DANGER! into the door of the church with a knife! Would that be too theatrical? Maybe the minister wouldn't like it. Oh well, she'd put a couple of bucks in the poor box, and who could complain? Now she should wear something frilly and light blue so it would be set off nicely against the coal-black paint of the church doors. . . .

"Back to Boston," she told her chauffeur. "It's dress-up time."

Meanwhile, Miss Earth was having a discussion with her class.

"I'm still thinking about the spider you accidentally crushed with the pumpkin," she said to Carly. "Is it a coincidence that a spider was on the other side of the apple Fawn bobbed for?"

"And maybe that thing I threw out the window was a spider too, remember?" cried Anna Maria. "The thing that got stuck on my sharpened pencil?"

"The place seems to be crawling with spiders," said Miss Earth, "which is perfectly fine as long as the spiders are harmless. But, my little naturalists, if these are for some reason dangerous spiders, we must use extra special caution. Pearl, I want to hear all about the spider you caught. Are you sure it didn't follow you to school, like Mary-had-a-little-lamb's lamb?"

"Absolutely," said Pearl. "My dad and mom don't like it much, so we keep it permanently in the terrarium. We propped the lid open with a pencil, just wide enough to slide a slice of pizza through, and also to allow some air for breathing."

"Pearl," said Miss Earth, "now I trust you, as you well know. But I need to ask you this to be absolutely certain. If we went to your house right now, would we find that spider in the terrarium for sure?"

"Yes," said Pearl.

"All right, I believe you," said Miss Earth. "Have you anything more to add?"

"Yes," said Pearl. "The day I captured it in Foggy Hollow, I saw some other ones. About five or six other ones, in some webs. I didn't *really* think they were Siberian snow spiders. I just said that."

"Thank you very much," said Miss Earth. "Class, I forbid you to go into Foggy Hollow until further notice. Am I understood?"

"Yes Miss Earth, you are understood," chorused the class.

"Then let's turn to our grammar books," said Miss Earth.

"But excuse me, Miss Earth?" said Pearl. "If I'm telling the whole truth there's one more piece I should say."

"Yes, Pearl?"

"I was going to bring in my pet tarantula tomorrow on a leash and at the skit I was going to have it onstage with me."

"Absolutely not. Forbidden. No discussion. You read me?"

"I read you loud and clear, Miss Earth," said Pearl sadly, and Sammy Grubb and the other Copycats looked grumpy. Their special little surprise dollop of terror was now x'd out of the script. They didn't blame Pearl for blabbing, under the circumstances, but they weren't happy about it either.

Class was dismissed, dusk began to gather in the corners of the sky, cold came in over the Vermont mountains, and down out of the night, right on schedule, swooped the helicopter carrying Meg Snoople.

She leaped out of it, live and in color, onto the Hamlet village green and onto the TV screens of forty million Americans across the nation. "Tonight we get closer to the mystery of the missing spider specimens!" yelled Meg Snoople into the microphone as the helicopter blades whirled. "Intense investigation has led us here, to pry the lid off a story so grotesque and scary you won't be able to eat your dinner. We go directly to interview a citizen of Hamlet,

Vermont, where we broadcast live during the rush hour."

But there wasn't much of a rush hour in Hamlet, Vermont, just an old man walking his dog. He hurried away when Meg Snoople began to run toward him with her cameraman behind her, although the dog looked interested in sharing a word or two with the nation. Meg Snoople was stuck. Then a girl came roller-skating through the leaves by the side of the road, wearing bright red reflector armbands. Meg Snoople dashed over to her.

"I'm Meg Snoople and this is live television, what is your name please?" she said.

"Lois Kennedy the Third," said the girl, frowning and sticking out her tongue at the camera. "Hi Mom, hi Dad. Thekla Mustard I hate you, I don't care if the world knows it."

"I have terrible news for Hamlet, Vermont," said Meg Snoople. "The dreaded Siberian snow spiders—the ones found in a glacier in the North Atlantic—"

"Yeah, yeah, yeah, they've overrun Hamlet, Vermont, we all know about it already," said Lois Kennedy the Third. "We've already accidentally killed a couple. Can I go for a ride in your helicopter?"

"You already knew about it?" Meg Snoople's jaw dropped.

"We figured it out. We're not dummies up here in Vermont, you know," said the awful girl, who in fifteen seconds was ruining the ratings of Meg Snoople's show. "But not to worry, nobody's been bitten yet. Did you get a permit to park that helicopter there? My dad's the local selectman and he'll fine you fifty bucks if you don't bother with the paperwork. Bye now. Bye America." Lois Kennedy the Third waved at the camera and roller-skated away.

"Clearly Hamlet is in a tizzy," said Meg Snoople. She wanted to interview someone else, to build the panic to a frenzy, but there wasn't anyone else around. They were all eating supper or milking cows or whatever they did in Vermont. "Everybody's hiding in their basements in terror!" said Meg Snoople, improvising. "Halloween is tomorrow night, and this is a Halloween nightmare come true!" She rushed up to the church door to stab her proclamation in place and finish this embarrassing failure of a live broadcast. The church door had been painted that afternoon, alas, and had a WET PAINT sign strung on twine in front of it. "Even the church is closed!" said Meg Snoople wildly. "This is Meg Snoople from Hamlet, Vermont, saying good night, America, and beware!"

Well, Meg Snoople's big scoop was a failure.

But people did watch it. Mostly they thought it was sort of funny; however, they did worry a bit about exotic spiders. Even the night janitor who washed the floors in the Josiah Fawcett Elementary School had turned on the television in the teachers' lounge to catch the news. With his feet up on the coffee table he grinned at the sight of Lois Kennedy the Third making mincemeat of Meg Snoople.

He wasn't the only one grinning. Attracted by the noise, the spider behind the movie screen had scurried down the hall and was peeping in the open doorway. It saw Lois Kennedy the Third on TV. With what it had of a mouth, it grinned. It had perfected its plan for murder.

17: Poison at the Pageant

The little red Fiat pulled into Hamlet, Vermont, an hour after the live broadcast. There didn't seem to be much to do at this point. The two nurses and the truck driver rented rooms at a boardinghouse called the Lovey Inn, which was run by a woman named Widow Wendell. She had a TV and a VCR in the parlor. "The national news was about Hamlet!" she said to her guests. "I taped it. Shall we watch?"

"How kind of you," said Pierre Montrose.

Widow Wendell popped in the cassette and pressed PLAY. Up came Meg Snoople again, screeching. "That's Lois Kennedy the Third she's talking to," said Widow Wendell.

The doorbell of the boardinghouse rang. Widow Wendell hurried to get it. She came back into the parlor with two more guests. "Full house tonight, and look who it is!" sang the widow gaily. They looked. It was Meg Snoople and her cameraman.

"You again," said Meg to Pierre Montrose. "What are you doing here?"

"Wanted to have a look around for myself," he said.

"And the nurse brigade? Are we expecting trouble?"

"Thanks to your fear-mongering, *yes*," snapped Head Nurse Crisp. "We'll see tomorrow what hysteria you've bred with your live-from-Hamlet nonsense."

Meg Snoople took herself off to her room, and soon after that the others retired to their rooms too, to toss and turn in the clutches of the imaginary spiders of their dreams.

In the morning all was chaos. The mayor of Hamlet, who most of the time was a highway repairman, went to work at the town garage out on Sugar Maple Road as usual. But a crowd of anxious citizens of Hamlet was waiting for him there. Meg Snoople was on hand with her camera, filming. Head Nurse Crisp, Nurse Prudence Lark, and Pierre Montrose came too, with Widow Wendell, who had shown them the way.

"Well now, everyone be calm," said the mayor, a calm man himself. "The only thing to fear is fear itself."

"What about deadly spider venom from before the dawn of time, Tim?" yelled a concerned citizen.

"Well, that too. But we haven't got any proof the spiders are really here, have we?"

Pierre Montrose spoke up and told the story of his truck crash eight weeks earlier. Everyone remembered that. "And the little Kennedy girl, she wasn't fibbing!" called Mrs. Yellow, Hector's mom. "My son Hector told me so!"

The cameraman zoomed in and out at worried faces.

Then Head Nurse Crisp had an idea. "We'll go to the school today and tell the children what to do in case of a spider bite," she suggested. "We'll set up a Spider Crisis Center at the school. With our professional ease and calm we'll help dispel fear. As long as there's a plan, people can cope. Start by soothing the children's anxieties and move on from there."

The townspeople agreed. Steadiness and courage, for the sake of the little ones. The crowd dispersed, and Mayor Grass left to paint new white lines on Hardscrabble Hill Road.

Pierre and Prudence went traipsing through the woods near where the truck had crashed. They came upon the gauzy remains of seven spiderwebs in Foggy Hollow. No ordinary spider could have spun such a strong thread or woven such a dense web. There were carcasses as large as toaster ovens, wrapped in dull pewter-colored cord and suspended like grotesque Christmas decorations. Prudence and Pierre held hands and gulped so loudly that the sound echoed back and forth between the walls of the ravine.

The schoolchildren in the Josiah Fawcett Elementary School, oddly enough, weren't overworried about the tarantulas. Lois Kennedy the Third's brash calm on coast-to-coast TV had given them the clue how to be about this: laid back. Besides, it was the day of the Halloween Pageant of Horrors at last, and tonight was Halloween night itself. It all seemed properly scary, nicely so.

The schoolchildren and a loving throng of available guests, mostly grandparents and mothers with babies and toddlers in tow, gathered in the auditorium after lunch. But before the kindergarten class could come on dressed as mice, the school principal introduced Head Nurse Crisp. Since the school didn't have a regular nurse in residence, everyone sat up straight and listened hard.

Head Nurse Crisp was glorious: soft-spoken, brave, funny, honest, and serious. She talked about spiders, about calm, about letting the nearest adult know if a very big spider was spotted, about how spiders are more scared of people than people are of spiders. Nurse Lark, sitting in the audience, was proud of her boss. Even Meg Snoople filmed a little for possible airing.

Then the show started. The little children were cunning as seventeen blind mice, seventeen blind mice, see how they run. . . . No one in the audience had ever seen such a sight in his or her life. They stamped and cheered and gave a standing ovation, and more than one mother of a kindergarten mouse had tears of pride in her eyes.

Some skits went on, and on; some were funny, some boring, some you couldn't quite understand. Finally it was time for Miss Earth's class.

But Mrs. Cobble stood in the wings looking at her watch, and shook her head. "Kids," she said to the girls in ghost costume and to the boys in black with their rubber spiders in hand, to Pearl Hotchkiss dressed up as Hubda the Magnificent and to Anna Maria as Miss Earth. "Kids, we got problems. That speech by that nurse person has cut into our time. We're running late. We'll have to cut one of your skits."

"Not *ours*," yelled the Tattletales and the Copycats and Pearl Hotchkiss.

"That's show biz," declared Mrs. Cobble. "You've got fifteen seconds to decide which it is."

"Keep 'My Fair Hubda,'" said Sammy in a steely voice.

"Keep 'The Haunting of Miss Earth,'" said Thekla, matching steel for steel.

"Let's *combine* them!" said Pearl Hotchkiss.

"I *like* it," said Mrs. Cobble. "A good trouper can improvise. Ten seconds to set up. Hit it." The kids leapt into action, dragging onto the stage the desks and chairs and card table to be Miss Earth's classroom, and behind them, the splendid spiderweb.

110

"Five seconds to curtain!" hissed Mrs. Cobble.

Seven Tattletales, seven Copycats, and neutral Pearl Hotchkiss all tensed up for their great moment.

So did the last remaining Siberian snow spider. It was clinging to a sandbag suspended high over the stage, ready for the kill.

Mrs. Cobble got the eerie music going. The lights dimmed. In came Anna Maria dressed as Miss Earth. There was a chuckle of appreciation from the audience. The real Miss Earth, standing in the wings, grinned and put her hands to her face in pretty embarrassment.

Anna Maria perched on the edge of the card table and took out her jelly doughnut. Then she tapped Miss Earth's little bell and said in a tone you could hear clear to the back of the room, "I wonder where my dear students could be today?"

The girls in their bedsheets and the boys in black began to swarm through the opening in the spiderweb. Everyone in the audience oohed and hissed. Pearl Hotchkiss, as Hubda the Magnificent, came through too.

"I am Hubda the Magnificent, the Original Spider Lady," improvised Pearl in a throaty croak. "I hear you got a pest problem in your classroom."

"I sure got pests all right," said Anna Maria/Miss Earth broadly. "Fifteen of them." Everyone roared with laughter.

The boys took out their plastic spiders. The girls began to wail their ghostly chorus of "We're the ghosts of former students, dear Miss Earth!" Hubda the Magnificent walked around, pointing out the jittering scrabbling spiders on their elastic threads. Miss Earth followed, stepping on each one with a high arching foot. The audience, revved up about spiders, responded with great applause.

At that moment the real tarantula descended on its thread. The kids on the stage didn't see it, but the stage lights picked it out and everyone in the darkened audience oohed and aahed at the wonderful special effect and clapped again. The tarantula's bristly body glistened in the spotlight, and it seemed to twitch graciously in a kind of aerial bow.

But it was confused. Its appetite was for Lois Kennedy the Third. But it couldn't tell which one was Lois, as she was draped in ghost costume like the other girls.

The spider swung back and forth over the heads of the ghosts, who now were doing their chorus-line kick step, while Hubda the Magnificent did a little soft-shoe. Then everyone bowed. The skit was over.

The girls took off their ghost-sheets so they could be applauded in person.

The tarantula saw Lois Kennedy the Third at last, at the far end of the row. It swung itself like a huge pendulum, its pincers ready, its poison surging.

Miss Earth and Mrs. Cobble, from opposite wings, saw it at the same time. Miss Earth was nearer. She didn't know if it was a plastic spider gone haywire or the genuine article. But she couldn't take any chances. She rushed onto the stage, waving her hands. The audience and her class clapped for her.

"Look out!" she cried. "Everybody duck!"

No one knew what she meant, and no one ducked. So Miss Earth pushed herself into the path of the attacking tarantula.

The spider smashed against the side of Miss Earth's neck and took a greedy bite.

18: The Trip to Harvard University

At first everyone in the auditorium clapped and cheered. But then Anna Maria let out her scream in high C, startling Mrs. Cobble so much that she dropped her eyeglasses. Meg Snoople leaped onto the stage with a microphone, shouting to Miss Earth, "Can you explain to America how it feels to be bitten by a Siberian snow spider?" The cameraman followed. Head Nurse Crisp pleaded for calm. Then Mrs. Cobble, hopelessly nearsighted without her glasses, pulled the wrong cord, trying to close the curtain. Instead of the curtain, a forty-pound sandbag dropped from the fly space above the stage, mashing the fleeing tarantula into spider marmalade. But the damage was done!

Miss Earth had slumped to the stage floor, a ghostly shade of white. Where the spider had broken the skin of her neck, a welt the shape of a snowball was growing. The students were in tears.

Head Nurse Crisp got to her knees and put her lips to the wound and tried to suck the venom out. The principal ran in front of the curtain and shouted, "Is there a doctor in the house?" Dr. Sternbaum came running up with her daughter in a pouch around her waist. She and Head Nurse Crisp agreed that Miss Earth wasn't to be moved. They shooed away Meg Snoople and told the children to go back to their seats. Mrs. Cobble tried to get the audience to sing, but nobody's heart was in it, and after a while school was dismissed.

"What's to be done?" wondered Head Nurse Crisp and Dr. Sternbaum. "Who is the foremost spider specialist in the country? How can we treat this poison when we don't know what it is?"

"The foremost spider specialist is Professor Harold Williams, at Harvard University," said Meg Snoople. "I can get him on my portable helicopter telephone."

"You can be *useful?*" snorted Head Nurse Crisp. "Then do it." Meg Snoople ran to obey.

Miss Earth's face was turning the sort of green that the inside of a yogurt container gets after more than three weeks. The principal went to call Miss Earth's mother and tell her the bad news. Around the edges of the stage door hovered the ghost-girls and spider-boys of Miss Earth's class, and the sobbing figure of pretend–Miss Earth in high heels, and Hubda the Magnificent.

In a minute Meg Snoople was back, her cameraman filming her mad dash. "Professor

Williams says to scoop up the spider remains and get them to him within the hour!" she yelled. "We can go there in my helicopter! He guesses that unless we find an antidote today, Miss Earth will—umm—depart this life—I mean—"

The children didn't pretend not to cry anymore. They wailed.

But Pierre Montrose was already hauling aside the sandbag, and the janitor was on the scene with his dustpan and a spatula from the cafeteria. He scraped up the tarantula gunk and plopped it in a Tupperware tub. Then Meg Snoople grabbed it and flung herself out the door of the school. It wasn't until she was climbing into the helicopter that she realized that Pearl Hotchkiss and Anna Maria Mastrangelo were at her side, and Sammy Grubb and Thekla Mustard not far behind, and the other children heading her way too.

"Get away," she shouted, "there's work to be done!"

"If anyone goes it's me, I'm the Empress of the Tattletales!" shouted Thekla crossly.

"It's my job as Chief of the Copycats!" yelled Sammy.

"This is larger than Tattletales and Copycats!" shouted Pearl over the growing noise of chopper blades. "I'm the only one who's tamed a Siberian snow spider! I'm a world expert!"

"And I'm Miss Earth!" screamed Anna Maria.

Meg Snoople began to see the dramatic possibilities of having two of the poor wounded teacher's students with her on this historic race against time. She dialed their home numbers and got permission from their mothers.

The cameraman dove into the back of the helicopter. The pilot pulled switches and twisted dials, and the helicopter began to lift off the green. In just a few seconds it was higher than the rooftops, higher than the church's slender steeple, and Hamlet, Vermont, began to look small and insignificant in the flood of forest and hills around it. The helicopter turned around and began to swoop southeast, toward Boston and Cambridge and Harvard University.

"What's this about taming a Siberian snow spider?" asked Meg Snoople, staring at Pearl.

"Oh," said Pearl, "I wish I hadn't ever done it."

"We should have stopped at your house and picked it up," said Meg. "But there's no time now. We can send the helicopter back for it if Professor Williams needs it."

Vermont became New Hampshire and New

Hampshire became Massachusetts, and almost before you knew it the highways and suburbs of the Boston area were flooding everywhere you could look. Meg Snoople pointed out landmarks beyond: the Prudential building, the Tobin Bridge, the State House with its gold dome. And there was Harvard just below, brick buildings and green quadrangles, on the banks of the Charles River, growing larger and more specific with every passing second.

The helicopter landed on the open lawn by the JFK School of Government. The cameraman jumped out first and got the camera going so Meg Snoople could be shot leaping nimbly and nobly out, with Pearl and Anna Maria stumbling after. Professor Williams was waiting. He took the specimen and ran to his lab.

"What can we do while we're waiting for your report?" yelled Meg Snoople.

"Go to Widener Library in Harvard Yard and see if you can find an English translation of *The Epic Verses of Hubda the Magnificent*!" he shouted. "Maybe there'll be some clues there!"

So Meg Snoople and her two young partners, still dressed in Halloween costume, hurried up the broad steps to Widener Library. At first the snooty bespectacled youth at the desk wouldn't let them in, since they weren't Harvard students or faculty. But Meg Snoople turned to her cameraman and snapped, "Put this twerp on national TV news as the snob who caused an elementary school teacher's death due to his fawning submission to Harvard protocol!" Pearl and Anna Maria, while they didn't like Meg Snoople much, had to admire her tactics. The student blanched and waved them through.

Up the stairs they ran, past the wooden drawers of the old card catalog, past the computer terminals of the new on-line catalog, up to the reference desk. "English translation of *The Epic Verses of Hubda the Magnificent*, tenth-century Russian, and make it snappy!" said Meg Snoople. The reference librarian catapulted into the stacks to obey.

She was back in five minutes with an eighteenth-century translation printed in tiny type in a heavy, dusty book. Meg Snoople sat down at a desk to read it, and Pearl and Anna Maria looked over her shoulder.

Finally Meg Snoople said, "Here's something," and copied out eight lines.

> *And should the cresting venom its dire*
> *target reach,*
> *No ailing soul can e'er survive if lifted*
> *from its bed*
> *And needs must die a horrid death of*
> *painful swollen head*
> *And limbs and lungs and ears, unless*
> *perchance maybe instead*

The sweet root of beet, if beet be sweet and
  within reach,
Or else whatever local grows, to take a bit
  of each
Rich honey, fruit, or nectar, and with
  careful caution leach
From each its sweetest essence—listen
  closely what I teach—

"It ends right there," said Meg Snoople, annoyed, flipping the pages back and forth, and reading the footnotes. "Apparently the sole surviving manuscript of *The Epic Verses of Hubda* breaks off at just this crucial point."

"What does it mean?"

"It says two things, near as I can make it out, but I'm no Ph.D.," said Meg Snoople. "It says under no circumstances move the victim from where she was attacked. It also seems to say that the sugary-sweet product of the local area contains the only known antidote. But what you do with local sugar, that's the important thing, and that's what's missing."

She closed the book with a *clop*. "Well, I don't know, girls," she said. "We may not have learned enough. Let's go back to the labs."

They crossed Harvard Yard again and went up the stairs to Professor Harold Williams' lab. Professor Williams came out with a couple of sizzling beakers of fluid in his hands.

"One more test and then I'll know," he said.

He went to his desk and found an old can of soda that still had some slosh at the bottom. He poured a brownish drop into both beakers. They both stopped sizzling and sputtering like sparklers and became clear, obedient, quiet liquid.

"It looks bad," said Professor Williams. "How'd you make out?"

Meg Snoople showed him the reference from the book of translated epics of the North. She told him what she thought.

"You're right," he said. "Amazing that old Hubda a thousand years ago knew by folk wisdom what I in my lab figured out this afternoon."

"Say it again so we can understand it," Pearl begged.

"The antidote can be made out of some mixture of sugars that the patient's own biological system is used to," said Professor Williams. "But the poison is a very intelligent one; it adapts to its environment. This Miss Earth can only be saved by a very specific antidote created just for her. If we had months and months we might be able to find the right combination of sweet ingredients native to Hamlet, Vermont. But without trial and error it is an impossible job to come up with something just like that in such a short time."

"Would having a live tarantula to examine help you?" asked Pearl.

"Not in the least, I'm afraid," he said.

Meg Snoople didn't even bother to film herself leaving Harvard with the girls to head back to Hamlet, Vermont, as the sun sank behind clouds in the west. There didn't seem to be anything that could be done. Miss Earth would be a fatality of the prehistoric Siberian snow spiders. What strange things fate had in store for people! She sniffled, in sad and feeling concert with Anna Maria Mastrangelo and Pearl Hotchkiss.

Back on the stage of the Josiah Fawcett Elementary School, Miss Earth's lump still grew, and her head and limbs and ears were swelling and turning a sort of purplish-green.

19: Trick or Treat

By the time the helicopter landed on the village green, nearly the whole town was waiting. The big crowd Meg Snoople had expected the night before was now on hand, but she hadn't the heart to shoot a foot of film. At last the human tragedy had come home to her, and as she got out of the whirlybird she hid her face from view, for the first time in her life.

Pearl Hotchkiss in her black Hubda the Magnificent gown and Anna Maria Mastrangelo dressed as Miss Earth alighted next. They stood blinking in the floodlights the mayor had set up. Around them were many children from the school, dressed in their Halloween costumes: ghosts and skeletons, ghouls and bank robbers, princesses and bunny rabbits and hobos and former presidents of the U.S.A. in rubber masks. Most of the grownups in the town stood waiting to hear the news too. Everyone was there, in fact, except for Miss Earth, and for Head Nurse Crisp and Dr.

Sternbaum, who watched their patient with increasing horror.

"It doesn't look good," said Meg Snoople. She stood near the people and told them that Professor Williams had offered little hope. Some people began to cry.

Pearl and Anna Maria joined their classmates. They told the sad story in their own words.

"What should we do?" asked Lois Kennedy the Third.

"What *can* we do?" asked Forest Eugene.

"In India we'd do *something*, even if it didn't work," said Salim.

"No one is suggesting we do *nothing*," said Fawn.

"But what?" asked Nina.

Thekla Mustard and Sammy Grubb, who rarely agreed on anything, moved away for an executive meeting on the steps of the Hamlet Country Store. After a few minutes they were seen nodding and shaking hands—peace, and no rivalry under these sorry circumstances—and they came back to their respective clubs.

"We have only one idea, and it's a stupid one," said Thekla. "But we might as well try."

"Try what?" said Lois Kennedy the Third.

"Trick-or-treat," said Sammy Grubb. "We're

going to trick-or-treat like we've never done before. Professor Williams said it would take months to come up with the right combination of local sweet effects. We figure there's no mixture of local sweet products like the mixture a kid gets in a Halloween sack every October thirty-first. We'll fan out, cover the whole town, trick-or-treat like there's no tomorrow. We'll meet back on the steps of the school in an hour and see what we've got. Are we together in this?"

There were fifteen silent nods. Fifteen unsmiling faces. Fifteen expressions that proved everyone understood—it was now or never.

"All right then," said Thekla. "Troops, move out."

And then began a trick-or-treat night such as Hamlet, Vermont, had never seen before. The dark-clothed spider-boys and the white-sheeted ghost-girls crisscrossed the town so fast that it would have looked, from the helicopter, like an old black-and-white TV on the fritz. Tonight the kids went for treats as if there were no tomorrow—everyone except for Pearl Hotchkiss, who ran home to get her tarantula and her little Spider Fun Factory for the molding of fake spiders.

An hour later they arrived back at the steps

of the school. The janitor let them in and opened the door to Miss Earth's room.

With great efficiency Sammy and Thekla organized the campaign. They had everyone dump their takings in a big pile in the center of the room. Then they sorted their loot into categories. Chocolate bars, sweet hard candies, sour drops, apples (candied) and apples (normal), candy corn, granola bars, and maple sugar candy. There were seven very smushed doughnuts too.

Meanwhile Pearl was heating up the little oven and lining up spider molds.

"The recipe called for sweets," said Anna Maria, "so we can just cross sour drops off the list." These were shoved aside. This left nine categories of sweets.

Forest Eugene and Sharday began to make a grid to figure out possible combinations of available sweets, but the real configuration was astronomically high. Some recipes, of course, could use four parts candy corn, say, and two parts doughnut, and skip chocolate bars altogether. From here on in, it had to be intuition.

They all took handfuls of ingredients and crushed them all up in their hands as thoroughly as possible. Each took a mold and squished the ingredients into it and baked it for five minutes in the Spider Fun Factory.

126

Since the oven could hold three spider molds at a time, it took almost half an hour to come up with fifteen sweet spider candies, made with local ingredients—a strangely colored set of beasts.

"We can't force Miss Earth to eat fifteen candy spiders," said Pearl Hotchkiss. "That's where my tarantula comes in."

She pulled the cloth off the terrarium. The tarantula looked around the room until it saw Nina Bueno, for whom it still had a strong yearning, only now the yearning had become murderous. Nina had to go hide behind the portable computer in order to allow it to calm down.

One by one Pearl lifted the candied spiders and held them close to the top of the terrarium. With each, the last living Siberian snow spider inched its way forward and put out a pincer. Perhaps it thought that these were a kind of gravestone to commemorate the disappearance and probable death of all of its kin.

But at the seventh candied spider, it backed up shivering and tried to hide under a rock.

"I think this might be it," said Thekla in a low voice. "Look, this is a somewhat mushy one. The proportion of doughnut in here must be a little higher than in the others. And doesn't Miss Earth eat a lot of doughnuts?

Well, she grew up on them, her mother makes them all the time, doesn't she? Okey-dokey, nobody lose your cool. Let's keep going."

Just to be sure, they tested candy spiders numbers eight through fifteen, but none of them provoked the dread in the captive tarantula that number seven had.

No one could remember who had created that particular candy spider, and maybe it was just as well.

Making sure that the tarantula couldn't escape, the Tattletales and the Copycats and Pearl Hotchkiss raced down the hall, solemnly bearing their candy antidote on one of the paperback copies of *Charlotte's Web*. It seemed only right.

Meg Snoople, Dr. Sternbaum, Head Nurse Crisp, Nurse Lark, Mrs. Cobble, Pierre Montrose, Mayor Grass, and Miss Earth's mother were all standing around Miss Earth, whose beauty had now become distorted by the swelling of various body parts.

Head Nurse Crisp, who among them had the most experience feeding the ill, took the candied spider in her capable hands. "At this point it can't hurt," she murmured, and Dr. Sternbaum agreed.

"Now we've got a little medicine for you, dear," said Head Nurse Crisp gently, although

Miss Earth was long past responding in words or tone of voice. "I'm going to open your mouth and put a bit on your tongue. If you haven't the energy to chew and swallow, just let it dissolve on your tongue, dear, and run down the back of your throat. There's a good girl."

With all the tenderness in the world, Head Nurse Crisp pried Miss Earth's mouth open with her finger and inserted the tip of one of the spider's eight legs. It remained there until Miss Earth's body temperature, which was 105 degrees now and climbing, melted the candy and broke it off. Head Nurse Crisp patiently tried a second leg, and a third.

"Come back to us," said Mayor Grass. "Come back, Germaine."

"Please," said Salim. "I only had you as a teacher for two months and everyone else had you last year. I need you still."

"We all need you," murmured her students.

"Honeypie," said her mother, "come back to us. This is your mother speaking. It's an order."

They waited. The clock in the church tower struck eleven.

At 11:15 Miss Earth's mouth moved a little, and they all held one another in suspense. Head Nurse Crisp fed her more of the candied spider. At 11:42 Miss Earth stirred. At 11:50 she was swallowing the candied cephalothorax, and at 11:53 she was greedily chomping at the abdomen. She finished off the pincers at 11:55, sighed happily, and just as the Halloween bells of midnight struck, Miss Earth opened her eyes.

"Trick or treat?" she said.

Epilogue: First Prize

Miss Earth recovered almost as quickly as she had fallen ill. The news made national TV, although with unusual modesty Meg Snoople played down her own important role in the medical research.

However, she did get a promotion and her own morning breakfast show.

Professor Williams was fascinated by the last remaining Siberian snow spider. After a long conversation with Pearl Hotchkiss, she agreed to allow the spider to go to Harvard. Professor Williams promised not to dissect it. Maybe he would even find a modern variety of spider it could mate with. Pearl Hotchkiss sent it postcards: "Greetings from lovely Vermont, U.S.A.!" She hoped it might escape one day and found a spider dynasty in some safe haven.

What the spider thought of all this is not known. But it did seem happy, as far as anyone could tell.

In Hamlet, Vermont, things got back to normal, except that Head Nurse Crisp quit her job in Montpelier and signed up to be the school nurse at the Josiah Fawcett Elementary School.

The first prize in the Halloween Pageant of Horrors went to the kindergartners dressed as seventeen blind mice. "Well, they *were* sweet," said Miss Earth, telling her class the news. "But in a way I wished that my class had won it, for I was proud of how you worked together on that skit at the last minute. Neither Tattletales nor Copycats." She looked at them with the quiet satisfaction of a true teacher getting the job done. "Maybe you're learning a little something after all."

"We worked together to save your life!" said Pearl Hotchkiss.

"There's no prize for that, alas," said Miss Earth.

But her students, gazing fondly at her, knew she was wrong. The first prize was right there in front of them.